DEJA VU

Formerly, UNDERCURRENT

LINDA FREENY

Ordering Information:

For orders and inquiries, please contact:
1-888-375-9818
www.toplinkpublishing.com
bookorder@toplinkpublishing.com

Printed in the United States of America

CHAPTER 1

Frank Damien wiped the sweat from his brow acutely aware of his aching shoulder, a souvenir of a bullet wound he'd received eight years ago on the streets of New York. He pulled on his ear lobe, an unconscious gesture revealing inner turmoil, and ran his fingers through his thick, black hair, his dark eyes filled with repulsion. He struggled to concentrate on the scene before him, a man and a mulato woman, dead from a horrible beating, entwined in an unnatural embrace. It was worse than bizarre; it was like stepping onto the set of a badly staged horror movie, the victims reduced to grotesque mannequins, bludgeoned to death with such force that they were unrecognizable.

Frank believed in the principle that every murder scene had its own flavor. This one left a nasty taste in his mouth that was all too damned familiar.

Tom Lawson, Frank's new partner, twenty-eight-years old and eager, said, "What do you make of it Frank? How in the hell did the killer manage to kill one of them without the other one fighting back?"

He's so young, Frank thought, almost naïve. Was I ever like that, or ever that young? I guess I must have been, ten years ago. Young, anyway. It seemed like a lifetime ago.

What Tom was saying was true, Frank concurred, experiencing a wave of nausea that could not be blamed entirely on his ulcer. The bedding showed only normal signs of disturbance, no more than you'd expect from two people sleeping. Almost as if the victims, Everett and Cleo Hale, had retired for the night and simply allowed themselves to be killed.

Frank sighed, willing himself to practice patience, not one of his outstanding virtues. This was Tom's first homicide. Excitement, rather than disgust for the nature of the crime, radiated from young eyes. "Try not to enjoy this too much, Tom. Let's see what the medical examiner and the crime lab crew came up with before we jump to any quick conclusions. Who found them?"

"Hale's kid, Derek Hale. He's outside. He says he hitchhiked in from Santa Barbara where he lives with his mother. He came to see his father, on a whim, or so he says." Tom nodded over at what was left of Cleo Hale. "The dead woman is the second Mrs. Hale. This is only a vacation home. The Hales lived in Beverly Hills. The officers who arrived on the scene first said the kid didn't look too grief-stricken.

Frank's eyes narrowed. "Any idea why?"

"No. No one's talked to him at length. He's a juvenile."

Frank found Derek Hale sprawled out on a chaise. He was ungainly and unattractive, suffering from a bad case of delayed puberty. His face was marked with one of the worst case of acne Frank had ever seen.

Frank didn't approach the boy right away. Instead, he moved across the sandy expanse to stare down at the rocks and the beach twelve feet below. He glanced back at the house and sighed ruefully. A million dollar hideaway. It must be nice!

He experienced a heady case of déjà vu. The house and its surroundings reminded him of another time and another place.

Frank was still staring back at the Hale beach house, envisioning another coastline, when a voice brought him back to the present. "Are you a cop, too?

Frank turned his attention to the Hale boy. He pulled a lawn chair up alongside the chaise, pushing the cobwebs of the past from his mind. "Tough break," he said, "finding them that way."

"Whore," Derek Hale spat out. "If Cleo hadn't gone after my father like a bitch in heat, maybe he'd still be alive."

Frank gave him a speculative look. Since it was too early to establish a motive, and robbery hadn't been ruled out, he wondered why the kid was so sure the brutal attack had been a personal one.

Derek Hale was only too anxious to enlighten Frank. "Cleo was young. Only twenty-two. And she was black," he added with disgust.

Frank drew in his breath. So much hatred. He wondered how much of that hatred had attached itself to the boy's father. He cursed himself. Over four years in this laid back Santa Barbara small town environment had made him careless. I'm slipping, he thought. I should have prepared for this encounter by seeing that a responsible adult was on the scene. He knew procedure required it. With the absence of one, anything relevant the boy said, or anything self-incriminating, would be inadmissible as evidence. All he could do was ask him what he had observed, or more importantly what he hadn't when he showed up here today.

By the book, Frank cautioned himself. "Is there anything missing that you know of?"

"You mean jewelry?"

"That, or anything else."

"I didn't check my father, but Cleo's diamond ring is missing."

Frank's interest peaked. "Why notice that item in particular?"

"Who could miss it? Six carats, so Cleo said often enough."

Frank resisted the temptation to cross the fine line he knew he was walking. Better to let the kid go now than have him say something they couldn't use later. "Go on home, kid. I'll get someone to give you a ride."

Derek Hale didn't seem to be anxious to leave. "Is that all you're going to ask me?"

"For now."

"Am I a suspect?"

"Do you want to be?"

"I don't know. I've never been a suspect." The boy moved closer. "But there are lots I could tell you."

Frank decided that Derek Hale probably had few, if any redeeming or appealing qualities. He beckoned to a uniformed officer. "Take the boy home."

Frank couldn't help wondering if the Hale kid was acting cocky for effect. Kids did that ever since he'd stepped foot in the beach house this morning he'd had the feeling everything here was done for effect, with a definite purpose in mind. But what purpose?

He walked back toward the rocks. Anyone could have climbed them and beat the last breaths out of Everett and Cleo Hale. Of course, there was a glitch in that theory. The beach colony employed a security guard.

Yet someone had gotten past him, either this way or through the front gate of the community.

As yet, a faceless killer. Possibly one as demented as the crazed killer back in New York.

"Frank, are you listening?"

Frank turned to face Tom Lawson. "Sorry. What did you say?"

"I said, do you think we have the first of many killings? Do you think Hale and his wife are the first?"

Now why would Tom assume they were dealing with a string of gruesome murders? Am I that transparent? Frank thought. I hope not. "We don't even know they are the first," he said out loud. "We won't know that until we get into the central information bank. We'll know a hell of a lot more when we get the medical examiner's report and the crime lab crew's findings."

He looked past Tom. The Hale boy was leaving. His kind made Frank glad that he hadn't had children. The kid was a nasty little bigot.

Claire had wanted children, he couldn't help remembering.

Frank took one last look around the Hale beach house. It was the most orderly crime scene he'd ever encountered. Everything was in its place. Even the bathroom looked like no one had used it recently. Bottles of cosmetics, aftershave, and colognes were neatly displayed on the marble counter top. Fresh towels were stacked on a tiered wall unit. There were three individually stacked sets of bath-towel, hand towels, and washcloths. The bathtub gleamed, as did the sink. It didn't look or feel right to him. But then nothing here did.

The first report on the Hale murders came from the medical examiner, Jess Griffin. He lifted his glasses up off the bridge of his nose. "They died between two and three a.m.," he told Frank. "They ate crackers and cheddar cheese and consumed several glasses of wine not too long before they were killed. I found six grams of a powerful barbiturate, Tuinal, in Everett Hale. I doubt he knew what hit him. Most of the blows were struck after he died from the initial head wound. Cleo Hale died about thirty minutes after her husband. They were both struck with blunt instruments, but not the same instrument.

Frank sighed. He'd known from the onset this wasn't going to be an easy case. The crime lab crew's finding verified it.

"You talked to the Medical Examiner?" Jack Serafin, from The Bureau of Investigation asked.

Frank nodded. "Then you know they weren't killed at the same time?" Frank nodded again. "They also didn't die together in that bed," Serafin went on. "Cleo Hale was killed in the bathroom, apparently after, or while she was taking a shower. The ends of her hair were still wet, so was the bath sponge. The crime lab crew found traces of blood in the drain between the cracks of the tile floor, and in the crevices of the hardwood floors in the bedroom, none visible by the naked eye. There are scuff marks on the bedroom door under the rug suggesting the body was hauled in there and carried to the bed. The shower curtain is missing. It was probably used to drag the body. We didn't find any weapons, and the only prints were those of a careless uniformed officer and the Hale kid. It suggests that someone wiped the house clean. Hale lent the beach house out a lot to friends and business associates. It should have been loaded with prints." He handed Frank his report. "It's a nasty one, Frank."

"There are no nice murders, Jack."

"I understand the wife's ring was missing. Did you find any other jewelry?"

"Nothing."

Frank pulled on his ear lobe. He remembered thinking how unnaturally clean the bathroom had seemed. "You said it was possible that Cleo Hale was in the shower when her husband was being murdered."

"I'd say so."

"Then why the hell kill her? If it was a burglary why not just take off?"

"I heard the missing ring was a six-carat diamond," Serafin said.

"Okay, so it was worth killing for. I'm not convinced this was just a burglary. Why the theatrics?" Frank said, thinking more out loud than expecting an answer to his question.

"Thank God that's your job and not mine," Serafin said. "I'd say you've either got a burglary intended to look like a grudge killing, or a grudge killing intended to look like a burglary. Your killer is either a moron trying to look clever, or a superior intelligence trying to look stupid. You could be looking for a psycho or a bungler."

Frank's blood ran cold. He'd come four thousand miles almost four years ago to escape the crazies. It couldn't be happening to him again. Or if it was, was he up to it? But could he run away? Frank had tried that once. It hadn't worked then, and it wouldn't work now. Some things you carried with you.

"You look tired, Frank," Serafin said, "You ought to go on home. There's always tomorrow. You married?"

"Not any more."

"Divorced?"

"Yeah."

"Me, too. Your idea or your wife's?"

"Hers."

Jack Serafin had no way of knowing he was striking a raw nerve. "Me, too," Serafin echoed. "In my case it was the job. Same for you?"

When Frank didn't answer right away, Serafin went on, "You came here from New York, didn't you? Ten years on the force back there, wasn't it? It must seem tame to you here."

"You kidding? After a day like today?"

Serafin smiled. "It isn't every day we deal with violence. Not like they do in New York or Los Angeles. Tell me, why Santa Barbara?"

"Because of days like today. I'd hope not to find them here."

"Then you think it was a psycho."

Frank could only hope it wasn't. The last psycho had almost cost him his sanity, and it had cost him his wife.

***

It was 2 a.m. Frank was sipping beer in his sparsely furnished bachelor apartment, not quite but almost on the wrong side of the tracks. For the thousandths time, and a nightly ritual for him, he was wishing he hadn't let Claire out of his life so easily. Wishing he'd had the stomach to stay and fight for her.

Frank crushed his beer can and reached for another. Damn this case. Why was Cleo Hale killed thirty minutes after her husband? What was the murderer doing for those thirty minutes? Did Cleo unexpectedly emerge from the bathroom, and did her killer drag her back in there to kill her, or had he walked in on her? Why create the illusion they were killed together in the bed?

"You're thinking crazy," he yelled out loud. "This is another time, another place, and just another murder case."

He turned the volume up on his small portable TV, as if to drown out an inner voice that chanted over and over again, "Quit, Frank. Quit this miserable job before it destroys you."

CHAPTER 2

M arian Hale stared out the bay window of her Santa Barbara hillside home. She checked her watch. Detective Damien had said he'd be here at ten. It was already fifteen minutes past the hour. Just then a car appeared. A dark non-descript sedan parked in front of the house.

Frank stifled a yawn. It had been a long time since a case had robbed him of sleep. At best he'd only gotten four hours, and most of them were troubled. He took a minute to appraise the house and the neighborhood. He wasn't up on local real estate values, but you didn't have to be to realize this was hardly a cheap rent district. Every house on the block was neatly maintained, professionally landscaped and tended weekly by gardeners. All the homes were large, each sitting on a half acre or more of land. Whatever else Hale had subjected his ex-wife to, Frank thought, hardship wasn't one of them.

He slowly exited his late model Ford thinking how out of place it looked amongst the Mercedes, Jaguars, and Cadillacs in the area. Just as surely as he himself felt out of place in Santa Barbara. His New York, big city mentality was a hard habit to break no matter how hard he tried. But had he really tried? he wondered. Truth was, in spite of everything that had happened there, he still missed New York.

When he'd felt the need to leave there almost four years ago, Santa Barbara was just a name on the map. What had attracted Frank here was its distance from New York, the fact that the population was only about eighty thousand people, and it was a coastal town with no nearby large metropolis. It represented sanity. God knows he'd needed something or somewhere that did. What he hadn't realized, but had found out in a hurry, was that Santa Barbara was a closed town. There was an existing moratorium on building to keep the town small and elite. It attracted the nouveau riche, anxious to rub elbows with old money, the snobs, and celebrities anxious to escape the Hollywood rat race. In contrast, Santa Barbara also attracted transients who slept on the beaches, the average seventy-five degree year-round climate ideal. Yeah, Frank thought, for a New York City street cop, it was a hard town to feel at home in.

Frank stared up at the house. He already had a pre-conceived conception of the ex-Mrs. Hale. He'd seen pictures of Everett Hale. He'd been good looking, virile, and fancied himself a stud. Marian Hale, he figured, would be stuck-up, used up, and an echo of the unattractive kid at the beach house.

The woman who answered his knock on the door was none of these things. She looked to be about thirty-five to forty. Her auburn hair was worn loose and shoulder length, framing a face that bordered on classic beauty. She wore very little make-up, and didn't need any. Her skin glowed, accentuating perfect cheekbones, the kind aspiring cover girls would kill for. If anything, the only detracting thing about it if you wanted to get picky, he thought, was that she had tired circles under her blue-green eyes. Frank had seen pictures of Cleo Hale. She too, had been beautiful, but more earthy. Everett Hale had been a fool, Frank thought. A damn fool to walk away from the woman who stared back at him.

"Detective Damien?"

He grinned. "Yes, Ma'am," thinking this was hardly an auspicious beginning, or a proper way for an investigating officer to act. He was glad he'd sent Tom to the beach community today to ask questions of the residents, the janitorial service, and the security guard to see if they could shed light on missing items and get their input. "May I come in?" he asked.

She opened the door wider. "Of course. Derek is upstairs, my daughter, Joanna, too. You said you wanted to talk to them."

"I also said you might want an attorney present." He looked around the step-down living room she'd led him into. It was empty.

"We don't need legal counsel, Detective. Derek told me about his performance yesterday. It was an act. Surely you realize that?" And at

Frank's uncompromising stare. "My god, you don't. You really think he might need to defend himself? To be treated like a suspect?"

A prime suspect, Frank thought, since the only prints at the house were his. Then again, that could just as easily point to the kid's innocence. Why wipe off everyone's prints but your own? Out loud, he said, "I don't know your son well enough to judge him, Mrs. Hale. If he's got nothing to hide, you have nothing to worry about. Can you call him in here?"

She hesitated, then nodded. "Certainly."

She moved out to the hallway and called up the stairs. Fifteen-year-old Derek Hale appeared, his eighteen-year-old sister by his side. Poor Derek, Frank couldn't help thinking. His sister, like his mother was a knockout. It seemed that all the attractive Hale genes had been exhausted before he was born.

Joanna and Derek entered the living room. Joanna peered at Frank curiously. "So this is what a detective looks like close up." She smiled over at Derek. "You lied, little brother. He isn't drab, and he isn't ordinary. In fact, he's kind of cute."

Derek had the good grace to flush.

Everybody took a seat, except Frank. His glance encompassed everything and everyone in the room before he turned his attention to Derek. It was a nice room, surprisingly pleasing to the eye despite its air of stateliness. The pictures on the wall were in the best of taste, and fresh flower arrangements added a pleasant and colorful touch.

He addressed Derek. "Yesterday you said you had some things to tell us." He glanced over at Marian Hale to make sure he had her full attention. Since her presence obviated a legal observer, she was a key element here. "I'm listening, Derek."

Derek shifted his feet. "I was upset yesterday. I don't know what I said. Hell, I'd just found my father and his whore beaten to death. I was grandstanding. Right, Mom?"

Marian Hale gave her son a sharp look, and one of apology to Frank. "You must excuse Derek. I wasn't there yesterday morning, but my son does have a tendency to grandstand. I have no doubt that like he did a moment ago, he expressed feelings that were very real. He told me he'd cast aspersions on Cleo's colored blood. It is…was," she corrected, "natural.

"Not me," Joanna chimed in, "and I rather liked Cleo."

"Only because her sister is the great Miramba," Derek said scornfully. "And because you hoped she'd help you with an acting career."

It was beginning to get out of hand. Frank took charge again. "So you have nothing to say to me now," he prodded Derek.

The boy looked over at his mother, his sister, then back to Frank. "Okay. You asked for it. Cleo slept around. I think whoever killed my father wanted her dead. My father got in the way, that's all."

Frank didn't explain that the murders didn't appear to have gone down that way, but admitted it was an interesting theory, one he couldn't afford to ignore. "Anything else?"

"No."

Frank sighed. The kid had had time to think things over, to rehearse any statement he made. Of course there was more. There always was. He realized he had probably gotten all he was going to get from the boy right now. "I'd like to talk to your mother. Alone," he stressed.

"Is she a suspect?" Derek asked.

"Derek!" Marian chided none too gently.

"It's all right, Mrs. Hale. It's a natural question." And to Derek. "Everyone who was close to your father and his wife is a suspect at this stage of the game. Everyone," he stressed.

Derek smiled. Leered really. Frank couldn't help thinking that thet simple statement had made the kid's day. What a warped personality!

Marian gave her son a fond but exasperated glace as he and his sister reluctantly left the room, looking backward as they climbed the stairs to their rooms.

She noticed the way Frank's feet shifted from side to side. "Forgive me, Detective Damien. Would you like to sit down?"

Frank nodded and took a seat close to the door.

Marian Hale smiled. "You have a lot of questions, I'm sure. Maybe I can make your job a little easier. My son tends to give the impression I'm the traditional woman scorned. That's not the way it was. Truthfully, Derek, and even Joanna, took Ev's infidelities much harder than I. But then I'd lived with them longer than they had."

Frank sat back in the chair. He craved a cigarette, but he didn't light up. There were no ashtrays in the room or any other evidence that Marian Hale smoked. "Why don't you tell me about your ex-husband, Mrs. Hale?"

"Ev and I were married for eighteen years. Some of those years were good ones. Then, like a lot of people, we seemed to want different things. When I first met him he was in law school. When he passed the bar, we moved to Los Angeles. He practiced law there for several years. They were lean years, because Ev couldn't seem to make up his mind what kind of law he wanted to practice. Always competitive, Ev was disconcerted to discover that in a city full of legal talent he was just another lawyer." She smiled in remembrance. "He wasn't the best of lawyers either, I'm sad to say. Then one day, an aging movie star, about to get stabbed in the back by her studio, wandered into his office. I'm sure she chose Ev because it looked like she could afford him. She was down on her luck, almost penniless. Ev turned things around for her, and she for him. Before he knew it, some of the bigger names in the business were calling on him, overlooking a lot of his flaws because they admired his forcefulness in dealing with studio executives. It seemed Ev had finally found his niche. He decided to quit law, per se, and become an actor's representative. Did you know, Detective Damien, that it requires no license, no formal-training? I didn't."

Frank shook his head. "I haven't ever thought about it."

"Neither had I. Suddenly, our life became one wild party after another. Young women, eager to break into show business, desperate for an agent, started throwing themselves at him. Ev loved it. Naturally, it didn't thrill me. I blamed Los Angeles for the change in our once orderly lives. I talked Ev into buying this house and commuting to the Valley every day. I quit going to parties with him. At first, he'd stay down there an occasional night, then it was two or three nights. Finally he only came home on weekends, maintaining a separate residence in Beverly Hills to go along with his new image. It was required, he told me, to not only look the part of a successful celebrity representative, but to live one."

"That bothered you?"

She smiled. "At first, but I learned to live a life apart from his. I had my children, I was active in the PTA here, and I joined the local art society. I stayed busy. I still do. It was odd, but it took me a while to realize that though I regretted the way Ev and I had chosen different paths, I was living a fulfilled existence. They call it adjusting, I believe. The last two years we were together we agreed to an open marriage. Unfortunately, for the children anyway, Ev wasn't at all discreet. I, on the other hand, was. I owed my children that. Ev and I agreed that if either of us found someone important to us, someone we wanted to marry, we'd get a divorce, but until that happened we didn't need one. Then he met Cleo."

"And you didn't meet anyone?"

She flushed. "I could tell you to mind your own business, but then I suppose you'd think I was hiding something. I did meet someone, but he wasn't the marrying kind, so he said, and I was, and am old fashioned enough not to want to live with someone. Later, I found out he was indeed the marrying kind. He was already married. Actually, I was lucky. He wasn't the man I thought he was."

There was no trace of self-pity, Frank noticed, just acceptance. "Did you resent Cleo?"

Marian Hale laughed. "Her youth and her beauty maybe. Not her place in Ev's life. By the time Cleo came into the picture I was beyond hurt and resentment. Disappointed?"

She was either lying, or an exceptional woman, Frank decided. "Let's just say I'm skeptical. Your son was pretty sure she messed things up for you and your ex-husband. Then, of course, there's the missing six-carat diamond your ex-husband brought for Cleo Hale."

"Ah, the ring. It rankled my children. They felt I'd been deprived. Look around you. This house that Ev maintained for us hardly comes under the heading of making do. As for messing things up for Ev and me, I think I've explained that." She ended further comment by asking him if he wanted coffee.

Frank declined.

"If you don't mind, I will."

"Please, go ahead."

She was gone for only a few minutes and when she returned she had a full cup of coffee in each hand. She placed one by his side on a small table. "In case you change your mind," she offered.

She sat back down, crossing her legs. Nice legs, Frank couldn't help thinking.

"Now where were we?" she asked.

"Your son's resentment of Cleo Hale."

She took several swallows of the scalding liquid. She grinned. "I drink far too much of this stuff. It's my fault that Derek's the way he is. I was so very anxious to protect him from Ev's and my separate affairs that I tried to keep up a false domestic front. Because I did, our divorce came as a blow to him. He was only twelve at the time. So much of his belligerent exterior is just that, a façade. How did you look when you were fifteen, Detective?"

Frank was taken aback by the question. "What?"

He smile seemed to wash away the circles under her eyes.

"Personally, at the age of fifteen I was an unqualified disaster. My teeth were crooked, my face full of what the kids now call zits, and I was too tall for my limited assets."

Frank raised an eyebrow. He couldn't imagine Marian Hale as ever being anything but perfectly put together.

"I see you don't believe me. It's true. I sympathize with Derek. Like him, I was a late bloomer. There are all kinds of discrimination, Detective, but none as cruel as discrimination against the ugly or the unattractive. He needs more from me than Joanna in the way of parental support, but then he always has. Joanna is very self-sufficient and independent. Before our divorce, Derek was popular with the other kids despite his ungainliness, because his father rubbed elbows, as did we on occasion with celebrities. When Ev married Cleo, it was as if he'd divorced Derek too. There were snide remarks from his peers, like "Colored lover.""

Frank raised his eyebrows again.

"I know what you're thinking. I saw it in your face earlier when Derek brought up the fact that Cleo was black. You were thinking that kids today are too broad-minded to be affected by interracial marriage. This isn't Los Angeles, Detective Damien. Santa Barbarans still hold onto old values. This town is full of snobs and bigots. Prejudice is, if not accepted here, quietly forgiven. Derek compensates for his present lack of physical assets by being a perfect beast. He's very intelligent, you know. He has an IQ of one-hundred-and-sixty."

Frank recalled that one of Serafin's observations had been the possibility of superior intelligence trying to look stupid.

"You didn't come here to compare IQ's, Detective," Marian Hale went on. "What else can I do to help you?"

"I'm not sure. There are some niggling little questions. Questions I don't expect you to have an answer to. You see Everett and Cleo Hale weren't killed together."

"Not killed together? Whatever does that mean? Derek said they were found dead in bed." She shuddered. "It must have been terrible for him, finding them that way."

"I know what your son saw, but there are disturbing factors to this case. Some I can't discuss. Was Everett Hale in the habit of taking sleeping pills? And why," Frank said almost to himself, "would Cleo Hale take a shower at two of three o'clock in the morning."

"I think I can help you with those questions." She looked puzzled. "They weren't killed together, you say? How very odd."

"You were saying you could help me," Frank prompted.

She continued to look thoughtful. "Ev and I were good friends before we were lovers, then husband and wife. After we agreed to live our own lives, we became friends again. It was a very special relationship, though some would think it strange. He used to come to me when he and Cleo were at odds, which was often. Their relationship was a stormy one. And yes, Ev did take sleeping pills. Increasingly stronger with each prescription. Sometimes he took more than a single pill. He was an insomniac. Every night he drank a few glasses of wine, then took a sleeping pill. He told me once, half joking half serious, that he and Cleo were having sexual time-table problems. Once he took his pill, or pills, he usually fell into a noisy sleep. Ev was a horrible snorer. Cleo always took a shower before retiring no matter what the hour. She never would allow sex afterward. It was a quirk she had. Ev hated it. He said it destroyed spontaneous sex."

"He told you about his wife's sexual hang-ups!"

"See, you think it's odd that he'd tell me something that personal. It wasn't odd, and if you'd known him, you'd know that it wasn't. Ev didn't make friends easily. We were together a long time. It's possible I was his only true friend."

Civilized divorces were a puzzle to Frank.

"Actually, my sympathies were with Cleo," she murmured. "Do you have any idea how disconcerting it is to spend time primping, using your most seductive perfume, and putting on your sexiest nightgown, only to find the object of your affections dead to the world?" She paled. "I'm sorry. That sounded horrible under the circumstances. Forgive me." Moisture filled her eyes. "Ev and I really were friends. I'll miss that."

It was her first real show of emotion. Frank guessed she was a woman who seldom lost control. The strain of what had happened to her ex-husband crossed her face only in unguarded moments, moments like this one.

He changed the subject. "Who will gain financially from Everett Hale's death?"

She looked surprised. "Not me. In fact if you're trying to give me a motive, it wouldn't have been a financial one. As long as Ev lived he paid generous alimony, enough to live like this. Now, God knows what we'll do." She frowned. "He did carry insurance for me and the children when we were married, but I think he canceled it when he married Cleo, paying alimony instead. With Cleo dead too, maybe anything he had went to the children. I don't know. Do you?"

Frank shook his head. "Not yet, but I will."

"There may not be anything to leave," Marian said. "Ev lived for today. He bought the house in Beverly Hills with what I think they call "leverage," a fancy word for little or no equity, and he continually borrowed against it. No matter how much money Ev made he always needed more. He mortgaged this house to the hilt to buy the beach house. It was an investment, so he said, but he wasn't fooling anyone. The beach house was a status symbol. An expensive week-end retreat."

"Did he have other assets besides real estate?"

"His business, but without him there'll be no agency. He had people working for them, but he WAS the business."

"Enemies?"

She gave a short laugh. "Where shall I begin?" She stood and paced the floor. She threw up her hands. " I hate this. He's dead, and he can't defend himself, but Ev didn't get where he was by being a nice guy. He stepped on a lot of toes, lured clients, or potential clients, out from under his competition and ruffled a lot of high-powered feathers."

"Like?"

She paused, seeming to concentrate on the question. "Several people, but Doug Beck seems to come to mind more than most. He discovered Miramba. Ev stole her away and signed her, and Beck was seeing Cleo at the time."

Frank wrote the name down. Doug Beck had lost a meal ticket and a girlfriend. That made him prime. He waited for Marian Hale to continue.

"Then there was Miramba herself. She wanted to make a movie she'd been offered. Ev had her booked solid on the concert circuit. She wanted out. Ev wouldn't allow it. He said she wasn't ready for the movies. She was livid."

Frank wrote down the name Miramba.

She sighed. "The list is endless. His brother hated him because Frank wouldn't bail him out of a financial scrape. He had to file bankruptcy. Jed hasn't been the same since. Of course there are others, but you'd do better to talk to people who worked with him."

Despite her inference that Hale had many enemies, Frank was interested in learning more about Doug Beck. "What kind of man is Beck?"

"My opinion of him isn't of much value, I'm afraid. It's only hearsay. I never knew the man, except through Ev, and his viewpoint was definitely biased. I know he resented Ev, and Ev never liked Beck either."

Derek Hale had said Cleo slept around. "Your son said that Cleo had affairs. Truth or fiction?"

"Truth. He overheard Ev telling me about it."

"Doug Beck?"

"Yes, they'd started seeing each other again." She cocked her head. "A good guess, or are you psychic?"

"No magic. Just a cop's instincts. Were they still having an affair when Cleo was killed?"

Marian frowned. "I don't think so. In fact Ev was the happiest he'd been in ages."

"When did you see him last?"

"A week ago. Eight days to be exact."

Frank stood. She'd obviously been expecting that question. "I guess that will do it."

He was all the way to the front door when he said, "Where were you when your ex-husband was killed, Mrs. Hale?"

"That depends on what time they were killed?"

"Two, three o'clock in the morning."

She smiled. "What you're really asking is if I killed the goose that laid the golden eggs. I saw the way you appraised both me and the house."

He decided he liked her. "Where were you between the hours of 2 and 3 a.m. the night your husband was killed?"

"I was home." She smiled ruefully. "No alibi, I'm afraid. I'd been to an art exhibition, stopped off at a friend's place, and then he drove me home. It was almost midnight when I got in." Her glance strayed up the stairs. "I looked in on Joanna and Derek. A mother with two teens can't be too careful. They were sound asleep." Her face lit up. "I guess that makes me Derek's alibi, doesn't it? He doesn't drive, and hitching a ride at that time of the morning would be almost impossible, and certainly verifiable if he did. Someone would remember a boy on the road at that time of morning."

"Does your son have a bicycle?"

"Of course he does, but the beach house is almost ten miles from here."

"Eight point three miles," Frank corrected.

She gave him a long hard stare. "Derek didn't kill his father, Detective Damien."

"Then he has nothing to worry about."

She wasn't ready to let it go. "Isn't it possible that it was an intruder? A transient? The beaches attracted them. Or some kind of psycho?"

The word psycho jarred Frank.

"Anything is possible," he said.

***

On the drive back to the station, Frank couldn't stop thinking about Marian Hale. She was honest to the point of foolhardiness, and refreshingly and disarmingly candid. He hoped for her sake that her son had nothing to do with Everett and Cleo Hale's death. She deserved better. With that thought came the knowledge that he not only liked her, but he was reacting to her much the same way he'd reacted to Claire the first time they'd met. And ironically, he'd met Claire while he was in the middle of an investigation.

Claire had been a breath of springtime in Frank's day-to-day crime-ridden existence. She was an apprentice journalist for a small newspaper, and she'd been jogging in Central park at the same time a man was being robbed and assaulted. She was the only witness to the crime. She was waiting for Frank and his then partner, Jack Gargon, when they arrived on the scene.

She was shaken by the experience, but in control of herself enough to give an intelligent report of what she'd seen. Unlike so many others, she made no attempt to avoid involvement.

She was small, almost petite, but that day she'd seemed taller. Because she was shaken Frank had offered her a ride home.

Home was a neat brownstone apartment outside the city. She'd invited him in, afraid to be alone, at the same time hesitant to let him see her fear. Frank wasn't fooled by her charade of false bravado, only drawn to her as a result. He'd known from the moment he'd seen her that she was special, everything he'd ever dreamed about but never dared to hope for. Gentility hugged her like a cloak. He found out but was not surprised, that she read literary books, knew fine art, and loved classical music. She was light in a dark world, and to him she seemed unattainable.

Their courtship was slow. He was terrified he'd lose her in one moment, kicking himself for thinking she could possibly be his the next. The night he'd asked her to marry him he'd given her details of his work, sparing nothing of its sordidness but minimizing the danger. "It's what I do," he said. "I don't know how to do anything else. I have no right to ask you to share a life like that, but I love you, and I can't not ask." He shrugged. "Of course, you have to turn me down. I know that."

He couldn't believe it when she'd said yes. He was twenty-nine. She was twenty-two. They'd been together five years and, when it was over, it seemed like five minutes. Five of the best minutes of his life.

CHAPTER 3

Frank sat slumped at his desk eyeing the blank page in the typewriter. When Tom Lawson come charging into the detective's room, he almost smiled, welcoming the distraction. He'd been trying to put into words his questioning of Marian Hale, but all he could think about were luminous blue-green eyes, a warm unaffected smile, and a vague resemblance to Claire that was drawing him to her like a magnet.

Tom plopped himself down in the wooden chair beside Frank's desk. "I think I got something, Frank." He pulled out a notebook from his inside pocket. "In fact I got a lot of somethings. Most of the people who live in the beach colony are permanent residents. They resent people like Hale buying property and letting riff raff, and I quote, "and every Tom, Dick, and Harry," into the colony at will. They're a snooty bunch for the most part who think that money makes them special. That's why they hired a security guard. Condo dwellers from down the way and day beachers were always climbing the rocks and walking on their precious sandy paths. It pisssed them off. The guard was hired to scare off sun worshipers more then sinister intruders."

Frank sat back in his chair waiting for more informative disclosures.

"Then," Tom smiled, "I met the woman who lives next door to the Hale beach house. Her name is Sarah Meadows, and she knows everything, and I mean everything about the colony. Who lives where, who is shacking up with whom, who is in financial difficulty, that kind of thing."

Frank smiled. This time the smile reached his eyes. He appreciated Tom's enthusiasm. A woman like Sarah Meadows could be a boone to an investigation, especially a homicide, assuming, of course, you could keep that type on track and away from rambling on about insignificant gossip. "What did she say about the Hales?"

"They fought like hell for one thing."

"Does she know what they fought about?"

"Yeah. Apparently they yelled loud enough for her to hear." He grinned. "But I wouldn't put it past her to listen in at windows. They fought about Cleo's affairs," he said triumphantly. "One in particular. Cleo Hale was seeing a guy named Doug. Sarah Meadows didn't have a last name," he added, regret in his tone.

"Beck," Frank supplied.

Tom's mouth shot open. "How do you know...?"

"Marian Hale told me. Apparently it wasn't much of a secret."

Tom looked crushed. Then, he brightened. "Did she tell you that Cleo and some man, probably Beck, used the beach house without Hale knowing about it? Sarah Meadows saw them together. At least Hale didn't know it for a while. His finding out about it was what one of their better brawls was all about."

"No, she didn't." Frank wondered why she hadn't. Marian Hale had implied that Hale confided in her about everything. Maybe he hadn't, and only wanted her to think he did. Frank hadn't bought their buddy-buddy relationship. It was unnatural. But it did raise the question of why Hale had bothered dealing in half truths and half disclosures where his ex-wife was concerned. Why tell her anything at all? They were divorced and owed each other nothing. "You said you found something else," Frank prompted.

"Marian Hale used the beach house on occasion. Sometimes she had her children with her, sometimes she came alone. At least once she had a man with her."

Frank felt an unreasonable pang of jealousy. He shrugged it off. What the hell was the matter with him? Besides, Marian Hale's love life wasn't an issue here. "Anything else?" he asked.

Tom consulted his notes. "Yeah. The security guard, Jim Parsons. According to Sarah Meadows, he's a lush. I talked to him. I asked him how anyone could have gotten past the gate. Apparently it isn't that difficult. All it takes after dark is a code number fed into a computerized box.

Theoretically, Parsons is supposed to check when he hears a car passing his cottage by the gate."

"Theoretically?"

"Yes. If it's a car he doesn't recognize as being to one of the residents, he's supposed to jot down the make and license number. If he's suspicious of the vehicle he's supposed to call the cops."

"And?"

"Parsons is an ex-cop, Frank. He knows the stupidity of covering up in a homicide investigation. I confronted him with the fact that I'd heard he drinks. He didn't deny it," Tom continued, as he flipped a page of his notebook. "He said, and I quote, "They pay me to keep people off the rocks and away from their little palaces, but they don't pay me enough to sit up half the night counting fucking cars." Tom closed the notebook. "In other words, most nights Parson is in a drunken stupor. The night Everett and Cleo Hale were killed was no exception. He saw nothing, heard nothing. Neither did anyone else in the colony. Then I doubt they'd tell us if they had. They're not the type of people to get involved."

"What about Sarah Meadows?"

"She's the exception. She'd love to jump into the middle of this case with both feet. But she didn't see or hear anything. According to her, although the Hales often had parties that lasted into the wee hours, the night they were killed it was just the two of them."

"Did she hear them arguing that night?"

Tom shook his head. "Seems it was one of their rare peaceful weekends."

It figured. Marian Hale had said the affair between Cleo and Doug Beck was over, and that Everett Hale seemed more complacent.

"So we're back to square one," Tom went on. "It could have been anyone. With Parsons admitting his negligence on the job, someone could have climbed the rocks, or gotten past the gate."

"Or used a password, or knocked on Hale's door, or been invited up there. I know. It's a wide open field. The guard? How come he enjoys such a good reputation if he's a boozer?"

"Prudence. And," Tom grimaced, "they're tight fisted. They don't pay him a whole lot. Seems they figured that if outsiders got the impression he was on his toes it would discourage intruders. It seems to have worked until now."

Frank looked thoughtful. "Now we have to find out if the murderers knew Parsons wasn't competent, or if they just took one hell of a chance."

Tom stared back at Frank. "They?"

Frank picked up a cigarette, lit it, and took a deep drag. "Just a hunch. But I think there were two of them."

Tom stared back at him expectantly. When Frank didn't expand on his statement, he said, "That's it! A hunch?"

Frank smiled. "For now that's all it is. Did you talk to the janitorial people?"

"Yeah. They were naturally touchy. Figured I was accusing them of something. I had them go over the house thoroughly. They said there was nothing missing as far as they could tell. All the stereo equipment, and televisions, five of them, are still there."

"So it's just the jewelry."

"Looks that way. So now what?"

"Tomorrow you go back to the beach. Work on Sarah Meadows some more. She probably knows more than she thinks she does. Just let her rattle on and see what falls out."

Tom made a face. "Thanks a lot. So this is what being low man on the totem pole around here means. What will you be doing?"

"I'll be talking to Doug Beck."

***

Beck lived in North Hollywood. His office was in Burbank. Since Frank planned to question Beck at his office, he notified the Burbank police station of his intention to question Beck. He was to meet with a detective, Ben Allandro, who would accompany him to Beck's office.

Ben Allandro was a big man in his fifties trying to slide through his duties until his pending retirement. He wasn't exactly thrilled to be dragged into the middle of a murder case, and that suited Frank just fine. The last thing he wanted was an eager beaver getting in his way.

The two men talked on the way to Beck's office. Allandro expressed open curiosity as to Frank's choice of an assignment area after finding out he'd been a New York cop. "Why Santa Barbara?" he asked. "Why the Sheriff's department?"

It was a question Frank was getting tired of answering. He discouraged further confidences, sorry he'd brought up the subject of New York at all. "Why not Santa Barbara?" he countered. "And what's wrong with the Sheriff's department?"

Beck's office was in a small building sandwiched between three-story office complexes. Frank wondered if Beck was on his way up, or on his way down.

Beck's secretary looked up as Frank and Allandro entered. They produced their badges.

"Is Mr. Beck in his office?"

She gave them a nervous smile. "He's busy, but I'll tell him you're here."

Doug Beck emerged from the inner room a few minutes later. He extended his hand. Neither detective took it. Beck dropped his hand to his side. "Come in, won't you?"

Frank took those few seconds to study the man. He was in his thirties, tall, blond, self-assured. His eyes were almost too blue, but women would like them, and everything else about him, Frank guessed. It wasn't too hard to understand what Cleo Hale had seen in him that made her risk her marriage.

Beck indicated two chairs by his desk. Accustomed to standing, neither detective took a seat. Beck shrugged and seated himself behind his desk. "I assume this is about Everett and Cleo." He raised his wrist and checked his watch. "Sorry to rush you, but I have an appointment in fifteen minutes."

"Cancel it," Frank said. The authority in his voice left no room for argument.

Beck visibly paled. He flipped the switch on his intercom. "Debbie. Cancel my ten-fifteen." He turned his attention back to Frank. "What can I do to help you? I hadn't seen Everett in a while. A long while, as a matter of fact."

"What about Cleo Hale?"

"Not since she married Hale."

Frank stepped forward and leaned over the desk. "You sure you don't want to reconsider your answer?"

Beck hesitated. "No."

"Are you very sure?"

Beck sighed. His eyes avoided Frank. "Okay, so Cleo and I were having an affair. It was over."

"How long?"

"We ended it two, three months ago."

"You knew Cleo Hale before she married Everett Hale?"

Beck came around to the front of his desk. "You seem to have all the answers. Yes, I knew her well. We were talking marriage."

"And Miramba?"

"Cleo's sister? We were talking career. Hers. I discovered her in a Hollywood dive. Cleo was at the club the night I caught her sister's act. I signed Miramba.

"I thought Hale did."

"He did. Later. Miramba's contract with me was a provisional one. My fault. I thought I was being clever. I also forgot the golden rule. Trust no one. Hale moved in on Miramba. He capitalized on a loosely-worded paragraph in the fine print. Cleo, by the way, was also a singer. She wasn't in Miramba's league, of course. Hale promised to make her a star like her sister. Instead, he made her his wife."

"You didn't fight for Miramba's contractual rights?"

"Of course I did. You have to remember that Hale had a law degree. He bluffed me, with Miramba's help," he added bitterly. "She threatened to sue me for misrepresentation. I caved in under pressure. "

"So you had reason to hate Hale?"

Beck gave a short brittle laugh. "Sure. Along with a lot of people. He was a lousy lawyer, so they say, but the son of a bitch was a master at screwing people."

"Like who for instance?"

"I hate to point fingers, but then," he smirked, "someone obviously pointed one at me. There's Marvin Peters, for one. He's a producer. He spent his last dime buying the rights to a property with Miramba in mind. Hale refused to let her do the picture."

"Why?"

"Who the hell knows? Hale got a kick out of ruining people. Look at this place." He indicated his office. "I'd signed a lease on a high-rise building a few blocks from here. I was betting on Miramba to elevate me to the finer things in life. I had to sublet." He saw the look in Frank's eyes. "I'm not the only one besides Peters whose glad I no longer have to contend with a man like Hale. Hale left quite a trail. I heard he even messed up his own brother."

"What about his ex-wife?"

Frank held his breath. For reasons he didn't care to explore, he didn't want to hear Marian Hale maligned. But the question had to be asked.

"Why should she be immune to Hale's malevolence? He was still married to her when Hale met Cleo."

"Where were you when Everett and Cleo Hale were murdered?"

"At a party. The kind only Hollywood knows how to throw."

"Did anyone see you there?"

"There were about three hundred people there. I talked to...I don't know, twenty, thirty of them."

"What time did you leave?"

Beck ran his fingers through his hair. "There you have me, detective. I got very drunk. I think someone put something besides booze in my glass. I woke up with my face down in the dirt in the garden area beyond the pool. I made it to my car without losing my insides. I didn't look at my watch. All I know is the party was still going strong when I left it. When I came home there was an old Barbara Stanwyk movie on television."

"You turned on the TV?"

Beck smiled. "Not when I came home. It was already on. If I don't leave it on when I go out my dog destroys my apartment."

Frank glanced over at Allandro. Beck's statement didn't seem to phase him.

"My dog is neurotic," Beck explained. "It happens."

"Did anyone see you come home who could verify the time?"

"Beats me. I practically crawled from my car to my apartment."

It was too pat, Frank thought. "We'll check out your story. I'll need the name of your hosts, their address, phone number, the names of the people you remember talking to at the party, and their addresses and phone numbers."

"No problem. I warn you, most of them were as blitzed as I was."

Before they left Frank also secured a list of people who had reason to dislike Hale. He hadn't been a popular man. He sighed. This could end up being a long case, and the bottom line could still be that Hale's killer, or killers, hadn't known him from Adam.

Frank and Allandro were closing the door as Beck's secretary spoke into the intercom. They heard her say, "Miramba called, Mr. Beck. She said to tell you that she will be able to keep her five o'clock appointment."

Allandro spoke for the first time since they'd entered the building.

"Want to go back in and ask Beck what that's all about?"

Frank shook his head. "It'll keep. Cleo's funeral is tomorrow. I plan to talk to Miramba after the service. She won't be expecting me there. Maybe I can catch her off guard."

***

Frank pulled the collar of his jacket up around his neck. People die and are buried every day, he thought. Why is it that every damn funeral I've ever attended is accompanied by overcast skies and cold winds? Somebody has to be buried in sunshine...somewhere.

He looked over at Tom. The younger man's eyes were riveted on a slender figure at grave side. It was Miramba. Frank glanced back over his shoulder. Uniformed cops were keeping back a crowd of curious fans, morbid onlookers, and a host of media personnel who threatened to turn this somber event into a circus.

Miramba was a phenomenon, an overnight sensation who was fast becoming a legend in a business that revered legends. Her first album went gold in weeks, and her second was already platinum with less than a few days on the charts. She'd won a Grammy for best newcomer her first year, and her latest video was so hot it sizzled. She was so flamboyant she managed to make Cher look tame in comparison.

Frank glanced over at Tom again and shook his head. A lot of help he'd be here today. He was here because Frank had felt sorry for him. Tom hadn't gotten anything from Sarah Meadows except a headache and vague innuendoes that meant nothing. "Don't send me back there again," he'd pleaded to Frank. "I try not to, but I tune her out after the first five minutes." The poor bastard needed this break today, Frank thought. Tomorrow I'll have him check out Beck's so-called alibi.

The service was over. Two burly men and a woman flanked Miramba on her way to a waiting limo. Frank stepped forward. He showed his badge. Tom did the same, his mouth half open as he stared at Miramba.

Frank did his best to rescue his young partner. "My name is Detective Frank Damien. I'd like a few minutes of your time. This ardent fan is my partner, Tom Lawson."

The woman behind Miramba spoke. "You could show some respect. Miramba has just buried her sister. Can't it wait?"

The two men moved closer to Miramba forming muscle-bound bookends.

"It's all right," Miramba said. She glanced over at the waiting crowds, and then looked over at the limo as if gauging the distance, wondering whether she could outrun the mob before they over-ran the policemen who formed a human barrier. "Can we talk in the car?" she asked. "I'll have you brought back here?"

Tom jabbed Frank in the side. Frank resisted a smile. Tom wanted to get close to Miramba like a lot of other red-blooded American males. Frank indicated the men and the woman. "What about them?"

"They can follow us in another car." She smiled. "You can be my bodyguards. I'm sure you're more than capable."

When the other woman began to protest, Miramba patted her gently on the arm. "It's okay, Marie. I'd just as soon get it over with."

The woman reluctantly gave way, but not before shooting warning looks at Frank and Tom.

Miramba took Frank's arm on one side, Tom's on the other. "Okay, let's make a dash for it."

Cameras exploded in their faces. When they made it to the safety of the car, Miramba gave the chauffeur orders to drive away.

Miramba removed the scarf from her head. She shook her long black frizzy curls. She was, Frank decided, the most beautiful woman, black or white he'd ever seen. She looked even better up close than she looked on television. Her skin was tawny, like silk. Her brown, almost black eyes were enormous. He glanced over at Tom. The kid was mesmerized.

"Were you and your sister close?" Frank asked.

"Sometimes. There was always rivalry between us. We were the only two girls in a family of nine kids. Whatever I had she wanted, and vice-versa." She laughed. "Cleo thought I wanted Everett Hale, so she married him. She couldn't have been more wrong."

"Why?"

She gave him full benefit of her dark expressive eyes. "Everett Hale was a first class son of a bitch."

"He was also your agent."

"Which is exactly WHY he was my agent. I was climbing. When you're in that position in this business, you either make it up the ladder or someone knocks you off. To make sure that doesn't happen, you need a son of a bitch like Everett to get you past the flack."

"Is that why you left Doug Beck?"

"Yes."

"You called him yesterday. Why?"

"How do you know I called him?"

"I was at his office when you called."

She looked thoughtful. She shrugged. "I had an appointment to sign with him."

Frank looked surprised.

"My agent died, remember?"

She made no pretense of grief. Frank had to admire that. Most murder suspects played it closer to the chest than that, and she had to realize she was a prime suspect. "Beck's office is hardly uptown. Surely now that you're a star he's out of your league."

"On the contrary. As a matter of fact I could make it without an agent. I'm getting more offers than I can handle. Who needs that kind of hassle? Besides, I'm past needing a son of a bitch. What I need now is an agent who'll listen to me and do what the hell I tell him, not the other way around. Doug does that every well. My sister almost made a career out of telling him what to do. I suppose you already know about him and Cleo."

Both Frank and Tom did. But they might not have. Miramba obviously wanted to be sure they knew. Frank purposefully let her remark go unanswered. "You're referring to the movie deal Hale wouldn't let you take."

It was her turn to look surprised. "My, you have done your homework. Yes. Everett was against it. He said the movie would ruin me."

"Like how?"

"There are some explicit sex scenes. It would mean taking my clothes off. All of them." She grinned.

"Now you'll do the film?"

"Of course I will. I happen to have a damn good body. I don't mind showing it off." She smiled, savoring the image of herself cavorting naked for all the world to see. "In fact, I enjoy showing myself."

Frank didn't doubt it. His neck felt like it was on fire. He unconsciously loosened his tie. "Who would want to kill Hale and your sister?"

She smiled. "You mean besides me? I mean Everett, of course, not Cleo. It's a long list." She gave him most of the same names that Beck had given him.

"Did you ever meet Marian Hale? Or her children?"

"The ex-Mrs. Hale? Once. She was very gracious considering the fact that her husband dumped her for my sister."

Marian Hale hadn't seen it that way. "She was bitter then?"

"No. that was the strange thing. If it had been me, I'd have clawed Cleo's eyes out."

"Maybe she really didn't care."

"That's what Everett and Cleo said."

"You didn't believe that?"

"Would you?"

There was nothing to be gained by pursuing Marian Hale with Miramba, Frank decided. It was obvious that all Miramba had was conjecture. "And the Hale children?"

Miramba wrinkled her nose. "Cleo brought them by to see me while I was recording my last album. The boy is a slimy little bastard, but Joanna Hale is a good kid."

"Where were you between the hours of 2 and 3 a.m. on the morning Everett and Cleo Hale were killed?"

She sighed. "I've thought a lot about that. Lying will protect my reputation, but probably hang me. The truth, unfortunately, isn't very pretty."

"I'd like to hear it."

She sighed. "I performed that evening at the Universal Amphitheater. There was a boy, about seventeen in the audience. He'd been to all my performances. He always sat in the front row." She smiled. "He was one hell of a good looking specimen. Blue eyes, curly blond hair, and a smile that melted your heart like butter. He passed me notes at the end of my performances."

"What kind of notes?"

"The usual. Like could he meet me after the show."

"And you let him?"

She shrugged. "It was my last performance. I had him brought to my dressing room. We talked. Then I went to a motel with him."

Frank thought about the burly bodyguards and the persistent woman companion. "Just like that? What about your friends back at the cemetery?"

"I sent them away. The boy and I slipped out the back entrance. I'd had him bring his car around."

"Where did you go?"

"A sleazy little hotel on Sunset. I don't remember the name."

Frank looked skeptical.

"Okay, it was the Top Hat Motel."

"How long did you stay?"

"All night. Afterwards, I had him drive me to a cab stand. I didn't want him to know where I lived. Kids like that don't understand one-night stands. Then I went home. I got there about 7 a.m."

Frank shook his head. "You're a celebrity, Miramba. Are you trying to tell me that no one worried about where you were all night?"

She flushed. "Those who are close to me know my habits." She gave Frank a pleading glance. He didn't respond to it. "Oh, for God's sake. My biography says I'm twenty-six. I'm thirty. With few exceptions I like my men young, Detective. Sometimes very young. It's not the kind of information I want publicized."

"What's the kid's name?"

"I didn't get it."

Frank raised his eyebrow.

"Believe me, I would have, if I'd known my sister was going to be murdered that night."

"Did anyone see you at the motel?"

"Are you kidding? I waited in the car. I wore dark glasses and a scarf on my head so no one would recognize me."

"Did your escort use his right name when he registered?"

She gave him an incredulous look. "I doubt it."

"So you can't prove you were there?"

"No. Short of putting an ad in the paper to locate the horny little bastard, which I won't do, I guess you'll have to take my word for it."

"I'm afraid it doesn't work that way."

She pouted and stretched out her wrists. "Are you going to arrest me?"

"No."

She withdrew her outstretched hands. "Don't leave town, right?"

Frank handed her his business card. "Call me if you think of anything that might help us. "He slid back the glass partition that separated them from the driver. "Take us back to the cemetery," he ordered.

When they arrived at the cemetery, Frank and Tom got out of the car. Miramba smiled up at Tom. "Does he ever let you talk?" and before Tom could form any words, she laughed melodically and rolled up the tinted window.

"I don't think she had anything to do with it," Tom said, staring after the departing limo.

"Well, that's your problem. And quit looking like a love-sick puppy, for God's sake. As far as I'm concerned Miramba isn't out of the woods by a long shot."

As they walked to Frank's sedan parked by the curb, Frank couldn't help thinking that he and Tom made quite a pair. Tom didn't want Miramba involved because he was infatuated with the woman and the myth that was Miramba. And he didn't want Marian Hale involved for reasons he didn't want to think about. If they didn't quit trying to eliminate suspects he decided, they, and the entire investigation were going to be in a world of hurt.

CHAPTER 4

Marvin Peters struck Frank as being the perfect caricature of a perverse human being. He certainly looked the part. His domed head was covered with sparse black and graying hairs, his eyes protruded like those of a goldfish, and a constant leer lingered on his lips.

Frank conceded his first impression and his quick opinion of the man could be clouded by the surroundings. They were on the studio lot, a closed set, the reasons for that were only too obvious. Two young girls stood naked by a brass bed. A man, equally naked, lay on the bed. Frank had to keep reminding himself that this wasn't a back alley porno movie, but the stuff people paid to see at their local theaters and the participants weren't extras. With the exception of one of the girls, the players were, if not household names, at least recognizable. Being here was like that time in New York, three dead flesh peddlers...forget New York, he cautioned himself, bringing himself back to the present, to the job at hand. New York was a lifetime ago.

Peters cautioned Frank to be quiet by placing his fingers on his thin, almost non-existent lips. The scene was brief. It would probably last less than a minute on the big screen. The girls tumbled on top of the man giggling, reaching for him, laughing playfully.

Peters hollered, "Cut. That was great, boys and girls. Take five."

The two girls and the man slipped into terry cloth robes and left the set without a backward glance.

Frank wondered why Peters had insisted on seeing him here, and decided it was the nature of the man. He liked to include everyone in his perversions. Frank nodded at the now empty set. "Are you so sure that's what the public wants to see?"

Peters slapped his sides and licked his lips. "Hell, of course they do. Naturally, we always overshoot, knowing some of it will end up on the cutting room floor compliments of some prick who believes he's God." He smiled. "But then there's always the European market."

"Is this what you had in mind for Miramba?"

Peters smiled, his expression lewd and ugly. He outlined a woman's curves with his bony hands. "Ah, Miramba. Now there's a number for you. The bitch actually auditioned for the part, right down to her bare skin."

The man is disgusting, Frank thought. "So you wanted her to do scenes like the one I just witnessed?"

Peters rolled his eyes. "But, of course. A Marvin Peters' film without T & A just wouldn't be a Marvin Peters' production. Tastefully done, you understand. I don't do porn, soft or otherwise."

"You could have fooled me. I suppose now that Everett Hale is dead you expect to get Miramba to do your movie?"

"Not expect, my friend, have. I closed the deal with her agent last night."

"You don't waste any time, do you? I guess that answers my next question. Hale stood in the way of your deal with Miramba. You must have resented him for that."

"Resented!" Peters spat out. "I had nothing but contempt for Hale. He got into the business on a fluke. He didn't understand it, nor did he belong in it." He smirked. " I have an alibi, Damien. I was with a very accommodating young starlet. She stayed with me all night."

"Can you prove it.?"

Peters snapped his fingers. A young man appeared at his elbow. "Paper and pencil," he ordered.

The items appeared in seconds. Peters wrote the name Stella Martelli on a scratch pad along with an address and phone number. "Call the lady. She'll be happy to verify she was with me."

Frank suppressed his disappointment. Peters was such an ugly human being, inside and out it would be a pleasure to take him in and charge him with anything. "Hale had enemies, I understand."

Peters shrugged. "Don't we all? It comes with the territory in this business. You found me, you'll find the others, I'm sure."

"No reason you can think of why someone would kill both Hale and his wife?"

Peters laughed harshly. "Hale, yes." He stroked his chin. "Cleo, that's another story. Her biggest sin, other than marrying Hale, was that she was ruthlessly ambitious. Hell, she'd have shafted her own sister! When Hale stood in Miramba's way on the movie deal, Cleo came to see me. She begged me to give her the part instead. Of course, I had to turn her down. She was no Miramba, except in the body department. She also auditioned for me by showing me her assets." He rubbed his hands together gleefully. " I love this job. Cleo wouldn't take no for an answer. She was sure she could wear me down in time."

"Did Hale know his wife came to see you about a part in the movie?"

"Not a part, my dear fellow. THE part." He shook his head. "I doubt it. She indicated she would leave Hale if he stood in her way like he was doing with Miramba."

"What about Miramba? Did she know Cleo came to see you?"

"She knew. I told her. I thought she'd get a charge out of it. She damned near clawed my eyes out, and made a few choice threats, like turning me into a eunuch if I even considered letting Cleo get near my picture."

Cleo supposedly had affairs. "Were you intimate with Cleo Hale?"

There was genuine regret in his tone. "No. I understand someone messed Cleo up badly before she was killed. The papers said she took several blows to the head."

Frank nodded, wondering if Peters was merely curious or leading up to something.

"She was a beautiful woman," Peters continued. "No one has a right to destroy that kind of beauty. Fuck, wasn't killing her enough?" he smiled. "I'd have loved to have slept with Cleo Hale. And she'd have been willing." He responded to Frank's stoic expression. "Not because I'm appealing, grant you. I know what I look like. She'd have given herself to me because I had something she wanted. Something she wanted very badly. The lady was a player."

On the drive back to Santa Barbara Frank gave a great deal of thought to Miramba. Cleo had wanted the part in Peters' picture badly, so he'd said. It must have been rough on Miramba knowing that not only had her agent stood in her way, but that her sister, who just happened to be married to that same agent, was looking for a way to ace her out. Murder had been committed for less reasons.

Peters' alibi with Stella Martelli checked out. She was a big woman, almost six feet of female splendor with the brains of a rabbit. A few minutes after he met her, Frank decided she was too dumb to effectively lie for anyone.

He checked his watch. It was almost four. By the time he reached Santa Barbara, Jed Hale should be home from work.

Frank pulled up in front of a small run-down apartment building on the outskirts of Santa Barbara. This was where Jed Hale, Everett Hale's brother, lived. A far cry, Frank thought, from the Santa Barbara hillside home and the Hale beach house.

Hale answered Frank's knock on the weather-beaten door. Green paint was peeling off it and the surrounding stucco revealed an older even more tired shade of blue, as tired and defeated as the man himself. He was gaunt. A nervous tick around his left eye made it seem as if he was perpetually winking. Statistically he was younger than his dead brother. He didn't look it.

Frank showed his badge. "May I come in?"

Jed Hale shrugged, the tic around his eye working more rapidly. He opened the door wider and stepped back to let Frank by.

It was a one-bedroom apartment. Frank could see the unmade bed through the open bedroom door. Dishes were piled in the sink of a ridiculously small kitchen. The place smelled of human sweat, stale cigarette smoke, and spilled alcohol.

"You came about what happened to my brother," Hale said matter-of-factly.

Frank nodded. "I understand there was bad blood between the two of you. Where were you the night he was killed?"

Jed Hale laughed harshly. "Here, in my little palace."

"Was anyone with you?"

"Look around you. Who in their right mind would want to spend the night in this place?" He kicked at the frayed couch. "I used to own better apartment buildings than this one."

"What happened between you and your brother?"

"The son of a bitch fed me to the dogs, that's what happened. I bought a lot of real estate in '79. No leverage, just gobs of deficit. Hell, I thought the well would never run dry. Back in '79 people were closing thirty-day escrows, putting property right back on the market, and making five, ten, fifteen, twenty thousand bucks. I held on. I was waiting to make forty, fifty thousand dollars a pop. I waited too long. The bottom fell out of the real estate market, overnight, or so it seemed. I was losing my ass. I went to Everett and asked him to help me out, to keep me afloat until the market got better, which was inevitable. He turned me down. Said it served me right for playing big shot. Everything I owned went into foreclosure. Everything. I filed bankruptcy. You know what that does to a man? It makes you feel small and dishonest and it tears your guts out. No one will take a chance on you because you're a bad risk. Then, if you survive it, you end up in a place like this one."

Frank had no patience with self-pity. "When did you see Everett Hale last?"

Hale shook his head. "Years ago. Why don't you just come right out and asked me if I killed him?"

"Did you?"

"I wish I had. I'd like to shake the hand of the man who did. Too bad about his wife, though. She was a looker. A bitch, but a looker. Personally, I think he made a lousy trade-in. Marian is a class act. Everett was an idiot to divorce her."

Frank was in agreement on that score. "Do you still se Marian Hale?"

"Some. She has me over to dinner every once in a while. She tried to help me when I was going under. She had no money of her own, though. All their assets were held in join accounts, but she tried. I was grateful for her efforts."

"What about Derek Hale? He seems resentful of his father."

"Poor Derek. He didn't take kindly to Everett marrying Cleo, but resentment of his father started way before that. Derek was puny from the day he was born. He was a premature baby. As an infant, he was always colicky. As a small child he caught colds. Everett had no patience with the boy, so Marian tried to make up for it by giving him special attention. My brother wanted a he-man for a son. Derek is an intellectual. Everett never learned to respect his genius. He considered his son a wimp." He frowned. "You don't think Derek killed his father? That's ridiculous."

"It's too early to eliminate anyone. I'm just gathering facts."

"You honestly think Derek could have…my God, that's the most preposterous thing I ever heard."

"Your conclusion, not mine, Mr. Hale."

Hale flushed. "I don't like you much"

"It's not a requirement, Mr. Hale. All I'm after is the truth."

"Is that all? Well, the truth is that Derek would never have hurt his father no matter how much he resented him."

Frank was getting tired of hearing that. He ended his questioning of Jed Hale on that sour note. Besides, he didn't see Jed Hale as a likely suspect. But then he'd learned a long time ago, that you never counted anyone out until the final play was over.

***

Frank stared distastefully at the frozen food section aisle in the chain store super market. Nothing looked appetizing. He studied labels looking for something edible that would microwave. He finally threw a frozen chicken entrée in his basket.

A voice nearby said, "You either have no respect for your stomach, your wife is away, or you're single. Which is it?"

Frank stared into Marian Hale's blue-green eyes. He glanced down at his basket containing the frozen dinner, chocolate chip cookies, potato chips, bean dip, and a six-pack of beer."

"I don't cook," he said.

She smiled, refusing to let him duck her question. "That's obvious." She placed a finger under her chin. "I'd say you were single."

Frank nodded, anxious to get away from her, but at the same time wishing he could say something to make her want to stay.

"I don't know if this is kosher or not, but I have steaks out at the house. Would you care to join me?"

Frank shook his head. "Thanks, anyway."

"You think I'm being forward? I suppose I am, and that's not like me. You see, I've never been a suspect before. Maybe you think I'll poison the meat." She laughed. "Now THAT would be incriminating, wouldn't it? Seriously, I'm alone tonight. Joanna went out on a sleep-over at the last minute and Derek is studying at a friend's house. She stared at the basketful of junk food. "It seems a shame to waste a spare steak. But if you're on duty..."

A detective on a homicide investigation was never really off duty. Regardless of that fact, Frank found himself answering, "No, I'm not on duty, and I'd love a home-cooked meal. You don't have to ply me with good food to ask me if I'm still investigating your son."

She blushed. "How embarrassing to be caught in the act of subterfuge." She bit down on her lip. "I am worried about Derek. He seems to enjoy thrusting himself forward as a suspect. He treats it like a game, and I can't seem to convince him it's a deadly one. I'm sorry if you think I was trying to compromise you."

Frank didn't want to see her go, but seeing her on anything that resembled a personal level was against all the rules, both departmental and common sense. He was smack dab in the middle of a homicide investigation, and even if she herself wasn't a serious suspect, her son still had a cloud hanging over him. He stared back at the unappetizing frozen dinner, weighing the prospect of an evening alone in front of television eating dinner on a tray, against an evening with Marian Hale. Good food, intelligent conversation...He stopped there. "Does that mean dinner's off?"

Her smile accentuated just how lovely she really was. "No. Of course not. I'll see you at the house. Shall we say an hour?"

Frank nodded, half eager, half reticent. With Marian he knew he was reaching for something he missed from the past. In so many ways she reminded him of Claire.

He stopped off at a liquor store and picked up a bottle of Beringers White Zinfandel because he didn't want to show up empty handed, and felt foolish for the gesture. He was acting like this was a date instead of a...What the hell was it anyway? He knew what it was for him, but what did she expect to get out of it except information? He'd given her all of that he could or would.

**

The first thing he noticed when he drove up to the hillside home was the "For Sale" sign on the lawn. When Marian opened the door, he handed her the bottle of wine. He gestured at the sign. "You're selling the house?"

She led him into the living room.

"Yes, I'm selling the house," she answered. "I have no choice."

Frank raised his eyebrow questioningly.

"I found out today that Ev left this house in both our names, and left my name on the deed to the beach house because he bought it while we were still married. With Cleo gone, everything else is left in trust for the children until they're twenty-one, that's if there is anything else to leave. If inheriting the real estate seems to make me seem rich, it's only an illusion. Fact is, I can't afford to live in this house anymore. With luck, I'll get enough from both houses to buy us something livable. Not on the hill, of course, but hopefully in a nice neighborhood."

She responded to Frank's look of surprise. "It's called equity, and I don't have it, Detective. Ev didn't leave much in this or the beach house. He borrowed heavily against both properties. This house should be easy to sell." She shrugged. "The beach house is a different story. I don't image a home where two people were murdered will be that desirable. I'll have to price it below market. Of course, I can't even start to market the property until your department releases it from their investigation. Do you have any idea when that will be?"

Now was not the time to tell her that Everett Hale had taken out a million dollar insurance policy on himself a week before he died. His beneficiary was Cleo hale. Now that she was dead, the Hale children's trust had grown considerably. He was finding reason once again to admire Marian. She was doing what had to be done and she wasn't delaying the painful process. Last week she'd had it all. A nice home, a quiet life. She was taking the changes well. At least she seemed to be. He shook his head.

"I don't know. Soon, maybe?"

"Does that mean you're close to finding out who killed Ev and Cleo?"

Derek again. She was worried about Derek. "No. But we'll find whoever did it. It's just a matter of time."

She shivered. "I hope so. Maybe then our lives can get back to normal. Every day seems to bring us a little closer to that reality, thank God. I scattered Ev's ashes at sea yesterday. There was no one else to do it except Jed, and he didn't want to." She sighed. "It was like closing the pages on a well-read book, knowing that you can never go back and read them again."

Frank frowned. He'd heard that Hale had been cremated.

Marian reacted to his frown. "The cremation was cleared by your department. They said they had all they needed from the autopsy. Did I do something wrong?"

"No. Why cremation?"

"Ev wanted it that way. He hated the thought of worms eating away at his flesh." She shuddered. "It's not a nice before-dinner thought, is it?"

There was so much Frank wanted to know about her. Not for the record, but for himself. "What do you do to keep busy?" he asked.

She laughed. "You mean because I don't work? Well, that will change. I'm looking for a job. Do you know of one?"

"Depends. What can you do?"

"Not much. I've been out of the work force for a long time. I'd hoped to find something in the art field."

"Do you paint?"

"No. I just know a good painting when I see one. Enough about me. Let's eat dinner before it gets cold."

Over dinner, which was the best meal Frank had eaten since Claire had left him, Frank tried to relax and not act like a cop. One question needed answering. "Nobody cried for Everett Hale. Or Cleo for that matter. Not you. Not your son. Your daughter. Hale's brother."

Marian laid down her fork and wiped her mouth on a linen napkin. She pushed her plate away. "What makes you so sure we didn't?"

"When I was here the day after your husband was killed, this was not a house of grief."

"You're right. It was a house filled with shock. Oh, we cared, but when someone dies of a disease, or even a tragic accident, someone who has been the center of your life for years, even if those years are behind you, there is a sadness that represents grief. When that someone dies violently, the way Ev did, shock takes the place of sadness. Then comes anger. The notoriety of the violent act attaches itself to you. You find that you're afraid to act in a normal manner because people are constantly watching for a reaction." She afforded him a steady look. "You know how it is. You must have encountered the syndrome before."

Frank stared down at his plate avoiding eye contact. She'd caught him testing her. It was indeed a fact that people who were touched by homicide often reacted the way she'd outlined, but few ever stopped to analyze the reason why. It was further proof of her ability to think things out, to see their true perspective. It was a trait he was beginning to admire more and more. It had been a long time since he'd felt he could talk to a woman and enjoy the experience.

After dinner they left the formal dining room and retired to the living room. Marian Hale curled up in the far corner of the couch, her legs tacked beneath her. Frank sat at the other end of the couch, his arm stretched across the back of it.

They had finished the Beringer. Marian brought out another bottle of wine. A beer drinker, Frank was starting to feel the effects of the wine.

"I should get out of here."

He hadn't realized he's said the words out loud until she said, "Do you have to leave so soon?"

"I could use some coffee. Would you mind?"

She stood up. "Not at all."

When she returned with the steaming brew, she said. "I get the feeling you don't do this often."

"Does it show?"

She laughed. "Yes, it does."

She watched him, her expression thoughtful as he swallowed the last drop of his coffee. "Don't you ever relax?"

When he didn't answer, she added, "Are you uncomfortable with me because I'm a reasonably attractive woman, or because I'm part of an ongoing investigation?"

He wasn't crazy about how the evening was turning out. He was supposed to ask the questions. "Maybe it's both, and you're more than reasonably attractive."

She flushed. "Why, thank you. I don't want to sound like a broken record, but Derek had nothing to do with…"

He placed his fingers on her lips. "I didn't come here to talk to you about your son."

He removed his fingers. The touch, unromantic as it was, was disturbing. He wanted her. That bothered him. Even worse, he suspected she knew he wanted her.

"Which makes me want to ask, why did you come here tonight?" Marian asked.

He reached for his coat. "I really do have to go."

"I'm sorry. I didn't mean to…Frustration filled her face. "It seems like I'm always saying I'm sorry when I'm around you. I really am glad you came. Maybe you'll come again."

The formality of not calling each other by first names, the pretense that they wanted to remain strangers, suddenly seemed terribly necessary. "I don't think so, Mrs. Hale."

"I see. Well, it's your choice, Detective," she replied, following his lead.

He was needy, and he knew it. He wanted to pull her into his arms, to feel her softness, smell her perfume up close, to know a woman's touch. This woman's touch. Need wasn't enough reason for taking advantage, and he knew if he acted out of need and impulse as his only motivation, he'd hate himself later. He stared back at her for a moment wishing he had less of a conscience. Then he turned and left.

***

Frank stood on the threshold of the bedroom. The room was shrouded in a mist that didn't belong in a closed room. A woman was tied to the bed. She was naked, her arms stretched above her, her legs spread apart. A man stood over her. He came closer. The fine tool he held in his hand hovered over the woman, taunting her. She tried to scream, but the cloth shoved between her teeth allowed only a muffled cry, like that of a wounded animal.

The instrument in the man's hand touched first one breast, then the other. Blood flowed freely. The tool turned weapon, moved down the woman's stomach. It stopped at the furry mound, then found tender flesh, and once more the woman's blood flowed onto stark white sheets. The woman's eyes opened wide. Tears ran down her cheek like a river. Her eyes pleaded for help, for relief from the torturous attack of her silent assailant.

The man turned to follow the woman's gaze. He stared at Frank. It was his nemesis, Michael Cordova.

Frank tried to move forward. His feet seemed to be encased in concrete. He was as helpless as the woman on the bed.

Then impossibly, the woman screamed through the gag in her mouth. The sound ripped through him. "Bastard" she yelled, not at her attacker, but at Frank.

It was Claire.

Frank sat up in the bed, sweat pouring down his face. He became aware of the phone ringing insistently at his elbow. It had awakened him, freeing him from the recurring nightmare. He was grateful for the intrusion.

Captain Cliff Markham was on the other end of the line. "Better get down here, Frank. There's been a new development that may have some bearing on the Hale case."

CHAPTER 5

Captain Cliff Markham was fifty-one years old, thirteen years older than the man standing in front of him. He'd been with the sheriff's department for twenty-three of those years, had bypassed retirement for a promotion, and readily conceded that Frank Damien had more raw experience in his combined New York-California fourteen years as a cop than he had ever hoped to see. He handed a teletype to Frank.

Frank read the communication. He felt a cold wave pass over him. It was from San Diego. A man and a woman, Glen and Kim Rowland, had been murdered in their beds. Beaten to death. The woman was white, the man, black. He handed the teletyped information back to Marks. "How much of it is the same M.O?"

"I didn't get all the details. I thought you might want to do that yourself."

When Frank didn't answer right away, Markham said, "You okay, Frank?"

"Sure. I just didn't get much sleep…nightmares. You ever get them?"

"Not as much as you probably do," Markham responded. When Frank gave him a hard stare he followed up quickly with, "You aren't thinking this is going to be like the one in New York, are you?"

"Why would you say that?"

"That was a psycho as I recall. This may be Santa Barbara, but we get newspapers and I read your file. Not all of it was in that file, was it, Frank?"

Frank sighed. "No."

"Want to talk about it…it goes no further than here, you have my word on that."

When it looked like Frank was going to pass on any more conversation, Markham went on, "They called him The Artist, didn't they?"

"Yes. He started with killing hookers, and when we thought we had a handle on it, he killed blondes, period. Then without warning it was brunettes, teens, pensioners. No common denominator, no income bracket, no ethnic group, no consistent thread, except that he always killed in groups of four and they were all female."

"They called him The Artist because of a strange calling card?"

"If you want to call it that." Frank already seemed somewhere other than this room. "All the women were marked with a fine pointed etching tool before he slit their throats. Every one of them bore blood-streaked patterns around their nipples and genitals which he inflicted on them while they were still alive."

"That's why they called him The Artist?"

"Something the media dreamed up after someone in the department leaked his trademark," Frank said, unable to keep the bitterness out of his voice.

"But you caught him?" Markham asked.

"Michael Cordova was a psychiatrist. He called us. Unfortunately, I was the one to take his call. He claimed he was treating someone who confessed to being our killer and offered to help us. Professional ethics, he said, wouldn't let him give us a name even if he had one. He claimed the guy just showed up at his office. We had nothing else so I went with it. Cordova and I were like glue for a while, almost like a partnership." Frank laughed, but there was no mirth to it. "I was beginning to like him. We had a twenty-four hour stake-out at his office, but the guy didn't show. It went like that for two months, and eight more women died."

"Surely you didn't blame yourself," Markham said.

Frank paced the floor reminding Markham of a caged animal. "Not then. Later. I can still see Cordova's face the day he smiled at me from across his desk, and said, "Surely you know by now, Frank, there is no patient, only me." Then he said that the thought of a policeman's wives was amusing, and did I know where my wife was."

"You arrested him."

"No. He blind sided me, and when I came to he was gone. He turned himself in the next day, declaring himself to be crazy. It took three men to pull me off of him."

Markham shuffled papers on his desk, looking for words, of what, comfort? How could you comfort a man as tormented as Frank was by nothing he could ever change? "I can give this case to someone else."

Frank had wanted nothing else since he'd seen Everett and Cleo Hale beaten to death. But who else in the department had his experience? Torn between sense of duty and self-preservation Frank finally answered, "No. It's okay. I can handle it."

"You'll let me know if you can't?"

Frank nodded.

"I'll trust you on that. You'd better get on the road to San Diego then."

"Is it all right if I take Tom with me?" Frank asked.

"I don't see why not. How's he coming on Miramba's and Beck's alibi?"

"I don't know. I haven't had a chance to talk to him." He gave Markham a wry grin. "If we're dealing with the same sick mind, it won't really matter, will it? I don't see any of our suspects so far at least, in the role of serial killer. Serial killers seldom have understandable motives. I think whoever killed the Hales knew exactly what they were doing."

Markham couldn't help wondering if Frank really thought that or just wanted to. Or, on a more troublesome note, if he needed to. "Could be you're right. Let's not close any doors. Okay?"

As Frank was leaving his office, Markham said, "Your wife was one of the police wives Cordova attacked. She survived it, didn't she?"

Frank didn't even turn around. "Yes...and no. When I came to, I rushed home like a man on fire. It was a cop's worst nightmare. Police cars surrounded my house. Claire was inside, a blanket wrapped around her. She was naked underneath it . She opened the blanket to let me see Cordova's work. A few days later she tried to hang herself. After that her only chance of putting what had happened behind her, was to put me behind her, because in his twisted way Cordova had made me a part of it."

Markham watched him leave, admiring him more than ever, sparing him pity because he knew that Frank wouldn't want that. " No wonder the poor bastard has nightmares," he mumbled to himself.

***

On the drive south, Tom told Frank what he'd found out about Miramba and Beck.

"I didn't find Miramba's boyfriend," he said ruefully. "You want me to keep looking?"

"Maybe. How about Beck?"

"It must have been a doozy of a party. Only a few of the guests admitted seeing him or talking to him. Then I doubt whether the others would have remembered talking to their own mothers. Most of the guests were stoned. No one remembers what time they got there, or what time they left. That includes the host and hostess." He grinned. "It would have been a great night for a drug bust."

"What about his apartment house?"

Tom shook his head. "Nothing. No one saw him leave the building that night, or come home."

"Which means his alibi isn't worth spit."

Tom nodded in agreement. "He has a wife by the way. Something he keeps under wraps. Her name is Sheila. She lives in England. Beck met her when she was here on vacation. They married, had a child, and then she decided she didn't like it over here. She comes back every summer for a month so he can see the kid."

Frank gave Tom an appreciative glance. "Good work. Beck told me that he and Cleo Hale were talking about marriage before Hale entered the picture. I wonder if Beck's wife knew about that. Just for the hell of it check on the whereabouts of Sheila Beck the night Everett and Cleo Hale were killed."

" Will do. I checked out Miramba like you wanted me to. She is thirty. And Beck's not the only one who hid a marriage. Miramba was married briefly a year ago. It was annulled after only two days. And get this, her husband who claimed to be eighteen was actually barely sixteen. It was kept very hush-hush."

"So where'd you get the information?"

"Her companion-secretary. I guess she figured it would make Miramba's contention that she was with a young stud that night more believable."

Frank stifled a grin. "Do you still believe Miramba's story?"

Tom flushed, aware that he was being gently admonished. "I don't know what to believe. If this double homicide in San Diego matches ours, what the hell difference does it make?"

Frank thought about his earlier conversation with Captain Markham. He nodded. "You have a point."

The San Diego authorities were happy to cooperate. The dead couple had only been married for a few months. There was a child. Hers. A boy of fourteen. Whoever killed Glen and Kim Rowland had beaten the boy badly and left him for dead. He was in intensive care, his life hanging by a thread.

The detective in charge of the case was named Art Lancombe. He shook Frank's hand, then Tom's. "You think we're dealing with the same killer?"

"Could be," Frank responded. "The Rowlands lived at the beach?"

"Uh huh."

"Was anything taken?"

"Too soon to say. We haven't done an inventory."

"Jewelry on the dead couple?"

"Wedding rings."

Frank nodded, more to himself than anyone else. The missing jewelry at the Hale beach house was one piece of information that had been held back from the press.

"If the boy makes it we'll know a hell of a lot more. Nasty business. The other woman was black, wasn't she?" At Frank's nod, he added, "If this is the same killer there's a good chance we're looking for a racist. That's going to go down hard."

"How soon before you'll know if the Rowland kid is going to pull through?"

"He made it through surgery. The doctors say that's a good sign. It'll be twenty-four to forty eight hours before we really know. Maybe longer."

"Then we'd better stick around." Frank said. "Can you recommend a good motel, Art?"

Lancombe laughed. "If your expense account is like mine, you mean cheap. There's a pretty good place just off the beach, close to where the Rowlands were killed. It's called the Sandy Shore Motel."

"Okay if we look around the crime scene?" Frank asked.

"No problem. I'll take you there myself. You can check into the motel on the way over there."

***

The San Diego dwelling where Glen and Kim Rowland had met their deaths bore no resemblance to the Hale beach house. It had been a permanent home, small, with two bedrooms, and only a single bathroom. You could put the entire structure in the Hale beach home's living room and master bedroom.

Frank eyed the ten-by-twelve bedroom. Blood stained the walls, the ceilings, the bedclothes. The Rowlands hadn't been killed with blunt instruments like the Hales had been. There was too much blood. It was the same story in the boy's bedroom.

"What do you think?" Tom asked Frank.

"I don't think we have a serial killer. At least not yet, we don't."

"Then you don't think the same person killed both the Hales and the Rowlands?"

Frank shook his head.

"Proof, Frank? Or another hunch. You ever been wrong?"

Frank barely hesitated before saying, "No."

"There's always a first time," Tom said, his tone slightly resentful.

Frank didn't blame Tom for his skepticism. How could he make him understand there was a special feeling in the air hours after a brutal crime, with the perpetrator or perpetrators leaving an unmistakable aura of their own. It took years of experience and a special knack that some never acquired or learned to comprehend. It helped if you'd lived on the cutting edge like Frank had. Something was very different here from what he'd felt at the Hale beach house, and not just the choice of weapon. Something more significant. The Rowlands could have been killed by one person, and Frank still believed that Everett and Cleo Hale had been attacked by two people. Two very clever people. He shook his head in disgust. An animal had left this mess.

"You're right," he consoled Tom. "There is always a first time. Lets see what the kid has to say if he makes it."

What Frank didn't say was that he was virtually positive that whoever had killed the Rowlands would kill again, and because of that one simple fact he would eventually be caught. They always were. It was only when they stopped killing that the crazies got away with it.

He wished he could be as sure that whoever had killed Everett and Cleo Hale would eventually fall into the net.

***

Frank and Tom were back in Santa Barbara. After days of nothing more exciting than tedious duty, events were now set on fast forward. Five days after the Rowland killings, Cleo Hale's diamond studded watch showed up at a Santa Barbara State Street jewelers. The owner of the downtown store, Jeffrey Malloy, had been approached by two men in their early twenties' wanting him to purchase the watch outright. He had instead, agreed to take it on consignment, using as bait the fact that he was sure he had a ready-made buyer he could call. The ruse had worked. Because they were transients, Malloy told them to call him back in a day or two.

Acting on police instruction, when the men called the following day, Malloy told them he had sold the watch, and that they should stop by his store to pick up their money.

Frank and Tom were waiting when the two of them made an appearance.

They had an air of modern day derelicts, the kind that filled the beaches and streets of small ocean cities like this one. Mostly, they came from comfortable middle class backgrounds, society dropouts rebelling against anything that resembled conformity.

They wore their hair long, a trademark of their rebellion. The one, a tall blond, sported a full beard. The other, shorter in stature, and darker wore a shaggy moustache.

Malloy took a step backward as Frank edged closer. Frank flashed his badge, motioning to Malloy, who handed him the watch. "Where'd you get this?"

The blond was insolent, irate. "We found it, man. What's the big deal?"

"You didn't steal it?"

"I told you, we found it."

"Where?"

The blond glanced at his companion who looked annoyingly unperturbed.

"At the beach," The blond man replied. "We were scavenging."

Frank held the watch up. The multi-faceted diamond band sparkled in the artificial overhead lights. "The woman who wore this was brutally beaten to death. You still want to claim you found it?"

The dark-haired man pushed his companion out of the way. "You mean those killings at the beach? You aren't going to pin that on us." He reached into his jacket pocket. He pulled out a man's diamond ring, a pearl drop diamond necklace, and one diamond earring. "We found these, too, but we didn't kill anyone."

"Can you prove it?"

The two men looked at each other. The blond shook his head. Perspiration began to bead on his forehead. The darker man took command again, his tone more conciliatory. "Honest, man. We found this stuff. We find a lot of crap. Nothing like this though. It never occurred to us…"

"Where were you the night Everett and Cleo Hale were killed?" Frank interrupted.

The two men exchanged wary glances. They made an attempt at bravado. The darker man spoke. "Who knows, man? One day is like the next. We don't live to a time table or a clock. We sleep on the beach most of the time."

"And sometimes you bunk out near the Hale beach house?"

"Not until recently. A few days ago as a matter of fact. We've been moving up the coast from Mexico. Someone told us the pickings might be better up here because the houses are so fucking exclusive. People like that are careless or just plain stupid.

"You figured someone was careless enough to lose a ten-thousand-dollar watch and the other jewelry you claim to have found? Come on now," Frank goaded. "Who in the hell are you trying to con?" he sighed. "I'm going to have to take you both in." He nodded at Tom. "Read them their rights."

Their names were David Simkins and John Manderell. Simkins was the blond, Manderell the brunette. They were twenty-four and five respectively. And they were sticking to their original story.

Even Frank's intense New-York-style interrogation, which Markham allowed after making passive noises that he didn't approve, wasn't having any effect in changing their story.

Because it was beginning to look as if they weren't going to break, Frank and Tom, along with uniformed officers and members of the crime unit, escorted the handcuffed pair to the spot where they claimed to have found their "treasure."

The site was at the end of the exclusive colony of homes where the Hales had met their death. The area narrowed out to a secluded cove protected against a sometimes vicious tide by large boulders. Because the ocean had been relatively calm, and because no storms had hit the coast recently, the tide had yet to reach the rocks.

Simkins and Manderell pointed to an area close to the boulders where they claimed to have dug up the Hale jewelry. Two officers held them back while a team of four men from the crime unit used sophisticated metal detectors and other electronic devices designed to ferret out foreign objects.

At the end of an hour there was a conglomeration of debris stacked on the sand. Aluminum cans, bottle cops, coins, the larges a quarter, and numerous other worthless objects, with the only real find the mate to the diamond earring that Manderell had turned over to Frank.

Frank, loathe to give up, instructed the team to concentrate their efforts further afield. They moved on down the cove.

Thirty minutes later there was a triumphant shout as one of the men held up a man's garnet ring and a gold Rolex watch. Both items fit the description of Everett Hale's missing jewelry.

More items were discovered. Several pairs of expensive gold and silver earrings and a string of pearls.

Frank was disappointed. There was no sign of either murder weapon, and where was Cleo's six-carat diamond ring? Was it a booty so valuable that the murderer had risked keeping it?"

It wasn't until later that day that the crime lab came up with the not unexpected disclosure that there were no prints on the Jewelry.

Frank conferred with Captain Markham. "I don't think Simkins and Manderell killed them, but we have enough to hold them. It might lull the real perpetrators into making a mistake if they think we're about to charge them with the Hale murders. Can you get the D.A to back us up? At least for a few days?"

"I'll see to it." Markham gave Frank a thoughtful look. On the surface Simkins and Manderell looked guilty. And there were two of them. He knew Frank thought there had been more than one killer at the Hale beach house. Though he'd seen no evidence to back up that theory, he trusted Frank's instincts, just as he was trusting those same instincts now by going along with Frank in believing they had apprehended the wrong two people.

When Frank returned to his desk, there was a message waiting for him. Marian Hale wanted him to call her.

She answered on the third ring. There was anxiety in her voice. "Thank you for calling. Derek is missing. I wondered if you could spare a moment to come over."

"How long has he been gone?"

"Since two nights ago. He was supposed to go to a friend's house. He never showed up there."

Frank muttered an oath. Just what he needed! Derek Hale, though not high on his list of suspects, was still a suspect. What bothered him was that he was sure it was no accident that Marian Hale hadn't reported her son missing until it looked like they had someone else to pin the Hale murders on.

He'd told Markham he was hoping to smoke someone out. He hadn't expected it to be Marian Hale in the role of protective parent. Since there was no official verdict yet on whether the Hale and Rowland murders were connected because the Rowland kid was still unconscious, Derek Hale's disappearance put him in the worse kind of light.

He was unreasonably angry with her. Enough to want to punish her for her actions.

"Call missing persons, Mrs. Hale," he reasoned. "I'll have my partner, Tom Lawson come by your house to follow up on it."

There was a momentary silence on the other end of the line.

"All right, Detective," she answered coolly. "I'm sorry to have bothered you."

The connection was abruptly severed.

"Fuck it," Frank muttered out loud. "Fuck it all to hell. He knew what was eating away at him like an incurable cancer was the undeniable fact that there were times, like right now, when his feelings for Marian Hale took priority over his casework on the Hale murders.

He had to make sure that didn't keep happening.

CHAPTER 6

It had been three days since Simkins and Manderell's arrest.

Frank was sitting at his desk, staring across the room, waiting for something to happen. His nerve endings taut with anticipation, he was more than ready when the call came in from the Burbank police station.

A woman had walked into the southern Californian station and calmly announced that the Santa Barbara authorities had arrested the wrong men in the Hale murder case. Then she gave them a name, Doug Beck.

The woman was Sheila Beck, Doug Beck's wife.

Sheila Beck's presence in the United States was no great surprise. Tom had discovered earlier that she'd arrived at Los Angeles International Airport at 9:23 p.m. the night of the Hale killings. Her story, when Tom questioned her a few days ago, was that she had checked into a motel five blocks away from her husband's apartment, and that she hadn't tried to reach him until the following morning.

Her story now was somewhat changed.

Frank sat in a small room at the Burbank station waiting for Sheila Beck to be escorted in. When she appeared she was alone except for Ben Allandro. He shook his head and responded to Frank's questioning look. "She didn't want a lawyer."

Frank waited until she was seated. He leaned forward in his chair. "My name is Detective Frank Damien, Mrs. Beck. Are you sure you don't want an attorney present?"

"Quite sure," she replied, with a distinctive accent. Northern England, Frank guessed. "I'm not guilty of anything." She hesitated. "Except perhaps a small white lie about not being at Doug's apartment the night the Hales were killed."

She was quite lovely, but considering Beck's appetite for great looking ladies, he wasn't surprised. Her skin, like that of a lot of English beauties, was unblemished. She wore her dark hair short, cut close to her head. Very few women could have worn it in that fashion without looking butch. Her brown eyes were large, doe-like, her teeth slightly uneven, which only served to enhance her appeal.

Frank leaned back in his chair. He studied her typed statement. "Have you read this over?"

She looked uneasily at the document. "Of course."

"Would you mind repeating your statement, Mrs. Beck? These things lose something in the reading."

She sighed. "When I arrived in Los Angeles, I called Doug immediately. He had no idea I was coming. I don't usually come over here until later in the year. He wasn't at home."

"Why did you come to the States?"

"I wanted to talk to Doug about our son, Kevin. It didn't seem like something you put in a letter, or talk about on the phone. I don't plan on bringing Kevin over here anymore. It's too unsettling for him. I want...I mean I wanted Doug to either give up his visitation rights or agree to travel to England to exercise them."

"Are you still in love with your husband, Mrs. Beck?"

She seemed surprised, "Does that matter?"

"It might. Pardon my frankness, Mrs. Beck. You just walked in here and turned your husband in for murder. That isn't an everyday occurrence. It leads me to wonder just how you feel about him. If you're bitter, it could cast a shadow of doubt on anything you have to say."

She smiled. "I see. No, I'm not bitter, Detective Damien. Whatever Doug and I had was over a long time ago. I'm sorry it ended, but neither of us is carrying a torch."

"Then why not get a divorce?"

She sighed. "Do you have a cigarette?"

Frank handed her a half empty pack.

She extracted one, accepted a light, and took a deep drag and blew out a trail of smoke. "Divorce in England is not just something you do on a whim. Not in my family, anyway. My parents are very old-fashioned. They've been married for forty-two years. I needed time to make them understand that Doug and I had tried, but it was better for both of us if we made our own way. Do you mind if I stand?" she asked. "I feel like a bloody convict sitting here like this."

Frank nodded. "Please, do what feels comfortable."

She paced the length of the room for a few moments, then stopped and folded her arms across her chest. "Like I said, I called Doug and he wasn't at home. I rented a car at the airport. I drove to Doug's apartment I was feeling bad about Kevin, wondering if I was being unfair to both my son and Doug. I wanted to talk to Doug, to get it over with before I weakened. I have my own key to his apartment. I let myself in. The television was going full blast. He leaves it on for the bloody dog. Can you imagine that? And Doug says we have problems! I hate that bloody dog." She ran her fingers across her brow. "I was really tired. I'd been eleven hours on a plane and there's an eight hour time difference between here and London. I lay down on his bed meaning to rest, but I fell asleep. When I woke up it was after four-thirty. I was angry because it looked like he wasn't coming home. That shouldn't have surprised me. I remember wondering whose bed he was in this time."

Hell hath no fury like a woman scorned, Frank couldn't help thinking. "Your statement says that your husband told you he killed Everett and Cleo Hale?"

"Yes."

"When?"

"The next afternoon. It's why I'm still here. I thought I could help Doug through this. In spite of everything, I feel like I owe him. Then you arrested the wrong men and everything changed." There was accusation in her voice. "It wasn't an easy decision, Detective...I'm sorry, I've forgotten your name."

"Damien."

"You see there's my son to consider. It's a real catch twenty-two. I could either let Doug and my son live a lie, or I could send his father to prison." She shuddered. "Or worse. How was I supposed to live with myself if I allowed two innocent men to pay for what Doug told me he did?"

Sheila Beck's ample bosom heaved up and down as her breathing became labored, her voice filled with stress.

"Please, take your time, Mrs. Beck. Just what did your husband tell you? And why confess his crime to you?"

"I've asked myself that question a lot. I think Doug was desperate, filled with guilt he couldn't handle. He said he couldn't stand the screams. He said they echoed in his head over and over again."

No screams had been heard. "According to the neighbors, Mrs. Beck, the Hales didn't cry out."

"Doug said they were violent, horrible screams. The kind you only hear in your head, or have nightmares about. Cleo was the worst he said. He told me she wasn't supposed to die."

A strange statement if she was quoting Beck word for word, Frank thought. "Then why kill her?"

Sheila Beck began to pace again. "He wouldn't say. Just kept repeating that she wasn't meant to die."

"Did he say why he killed them?"

"No. I asked him that. He just stared at me. Past me, really."

"Did you know that your husband was having an affair with Cleo Hale?"

She raised her head. Her eyes met Frank's. "Yes. That was a while ago. It was over between them."

Frank sighed inwardly. Sheila Beck might not be carrying a torch, but he'd bet money that more than just a small flame still flickered. "And the weapon? Did he say what weapon he used?"

Frank held his breath. Her next statement was a crucial one. If Beck had named the weapon used, they had him.

She frowned. "Weapon? I'm sorry, he didn't say. Just that he'd beaten them. Beaten them until they…it must have been awful."

Frank wondered if her concern was for the Hales, or for Doug Beck. He swore under his breath. Identifying the weapons would have been icing on the cake. "Does your husband know that you planned on coming to see us?"

"No. the day after he told me about killing the Hales, he denied everything. He said it was a sick joke. I wanted to believe him. That he couldn't…I mean, you live with someone, you have his child…" She gave

Frank a pleading glance. "How can you do that and not know a man is capable of murder?"

"What makes you believe his original confession wasn't a joke?"

"His eyes. Doug never could hide the truth from me just so long as he was looking right at me. He was looking right at me the day he told me he'd killed those people." She swallowed. "I'm sorry. I'm not handling this very well."

Frank rubbed his cheek with his index finger. "You know we can't make you testify against your husband."

"Yes, I know. Quite honestly, I don't even know if I could."

Her statement wasn't unexpected. Even if she could or would testify, Beck would block her from doing it.

"Don't worry, Mrs. Beck. If he's really guilty we'll find a way to get him."

"I'm afraid. What if Doug is innocent?"

"If you believed that, you wouldn't be here."

She lowered her head. Frank steeled himself not to feel sorry for her. It was an emotion he couldn't afford.

Frank wore a path in front of Captain Markham's desk. He related the events of his session with Sheila Beck. When he was done he threw his hands up in the air. "Damn it, Cliff, I believe her. I believe Beck was there at the beach house the night Everett and Cleo Hale were killed. And I believe he either did it, or helped someone else kill them."

Cliff Markham waited for Frank to vent his frustration.

"Damn it, Cliff," Frank said again. "I wish he'd confessed to someone other than his wife." He pulled on his ear lobe. "We can't use her statement against him, any smart attorney will tell him that. We need to back up her statement with hard evidence."

Markham sympathized with Frank's frustration. "It's a tough one. I'll go with you on whatever you want to do, Frank?"

Frank shook his head. "Gee, thanks a whole hell of a lot, Cliff. You know we have to bring him in for questioning. I just wish we had something more solid to go on than Sheila Beck's statement. We're going to have to build a case without her testimony. What we need is motive and opportunity. I think Tom and I should question the guests at the party more thoroughly. Maybe someone will remember what time Beck really left. I'd like to show his picture around the beach colony. Maybe someone saw him there that night."

"I thought it had been established that no one saw any strangers there that night."

Frank sighed. "They didn't, but it's worth another try. What's the chances of getting a search warrant for Beck's apartment and his office? He may have gotten careless. Hung onto something that will bury him. We need to talk at length to Beck's receptionist and Hale's staff."

"I think we have cause to ask for a warrant. I'll get to work on it, and I'll continue to hold Simkins and Manderell until you're ready to make your play with Beck."

"Thanks. And , Cliff?"

"Yes?"

"Wish me luck. Ever since the night of the Hale murders I've been reminded of Cordova, and I don't know why. I should have told you that, that day in your office. I didn't want you to think I wasn't up to it."

"I would never think that, Frank. You're too good a cop. I think you'd holla' uncle all by yourself if you were in too deep. Besides, Cordova was a psycho."

"Thanks for the vote of confidence." Frank stared thoughtfully past him. "Yeah, Cordova was a psycho. Stupid, isn't it? Beck's not a bit like Cordova."

"Then what's bothering you?"

"Beats the hell out of me. Cordova was clever. Under normal circumstances he might have been considered a genius. Beck's clever, too. He's just not crazy. Or if he is, he's crazy like a fox. Maybe he sent his wife to us knowing we couldn't touch him with her statement."

"Risky business, that, don't you think? It's diverted our attention away from everyone else and put him in the spotlight."

"Maybe that's what's bothering me."

Markham said, "They put Cordova away for a long time, didn't they?"

Frank nodded. "He's in a nut house. Did you know I wanted him dead? I wanted to see him swing from a rope, die in an electric chair, or eat gas. I wanted him dead so badly that it almost drove me crazy when it didn't happen."

As in their last conversation about Cordova, Markham knew there was nothing he could say or do to help Frank with a past he couldn't leave behind. No one could. So he said nothing.

It was just as Tom had said. The party Beck claimed to have attended until late in the morning was a drug dealer's paradise. Though no one was openly admitting they were stoned, nobody could shed light on what time when Beck had left.

Their last stop was the home of Josh and Evelyn Pine, the hosts of the party. Frank scanned the guest list. "Are you sure this is a complete list of your guests that night, Mr. and Mrs. Pine?"

Josh Pine concentrated on the list of names. He shook his head. "We get gate crashers. I couldn't possibly begin to say who might have just walked in off the street."

He passed the list to his wife. Evelyn Pine shrugged and started to hand it back to Frank, then stopped. "Of course! I forgot. Penny Downing! Remember, Josh? We didn't invite her because we thought she was still in Europe, but then Maria Escobar told us she was back. We called Penny personally to ask her to the party, though I don't know why, she's such a drag. Do you know if she showed up, Honey?"

"No, but then it was one of those parties." He smiled apologetically at Frank and Tom. "Sorry."

"If you think of anything," Frank said, "call me. Perhaps you can give me Penny Downing's address."

"Of course." Evelyn Pine answered.

Frank accepted the address from her. "Thanks. Take some advice Mr. and Mrs. Pine. If I was a narc, I'd make keeping an eye on the two of you a priority."

Pine gave him a speculative glance, started to say something, and thought better of it.

***

Penny Downing was not what Frank had expected. He'd assumed she'd be another Hollywood bubble head. Instead, she was a conservative young woman in her early twenties who was putting herself through college and paying the rent with a part-time job as a waitress, and an occasional TV commercial. She had gotten on the Pine party guest list because of her association with Randy Maharis, a popular young actor. She'd been in Europe with him on location prior to the Pine party. She'd left Europe and Maharis so as to catch up on her studies.

She was refreshingly frank and straightforward. "I told you about my job because I don't want you to think I let Randy pay my bills. A lot of people think he does. Like Josh and Evelyn Pine." She shivered. "I hate their parties. To be fair, on the other side of the coin, they aren't exactly crazy about me either. They think I'm a prude because I don't like to fill my body with drugs. They only ask me to their gatherings because they're afraid of upsetting Randy. The night of the party you're asking about, I wasn't going to go. Then Randy called from Europe. I told him about the invitation. He urged me to go. He said it would be good for me." She shuddered. "God knows why. I put in an appearance for his sake."

"How long did you stay?" Frank asked.

"About an hour."

"I don't suppose you saw this man."

Penny studied Beck's picture. "Yes, I did. His name is Doug something or other. Randy introduced us once. I think he's trying to get Randy to sign with his agency."

Frank put the picture back inside his jacket pocket. "Was he still there when you left the party?"

"No, he wasn't."

"You seem very sure. There were a lot of people at the party. Why notice the activities of one man?"

"Because he stood out. I think he and I were the only sober people there."

"Did you talk to him?"

"No. I might have, except he left."

"When?"

"Right before I did."

"What time was that?"

"I'm not sure exactly. Is it important?"

"Damned important, Miss Downing. Do you have any idea what time he left?"

"It was around ten."

"How can you be sure he left? Isn't it possible he just disappeared into the crowd, the garden, or another part of the house?"

She looked distinctly annoyed. "No. I saw him get in his car, a sports model, a Jaguar, I believe, and then he drove away."

"And you're sure he was sober?"

"He looked it."

Frank smiled in encouragement. "This is very important. Why are you so sure it was around ten? Couldn't it have been much later?"

She vigorously shook her head. "No. My phone was ringing when I walked in the door of my apartment. It was Randy. He was having second thoughts about my attending the party. There's an eight hour time difference. I looked at my watch. I teased him about calling me so early in the morning. It was six-thirty in France."

"And you'll testify to the fact that Doug Beck left the party about ten o'clock?"

"I suppose so. What's this all about?"

"Murder, Miss Downing. It's about murder."

***

Frank took on Hale's staff while Tom tackled Beck's secretary. She had nothing to say, nothing helpful at least.

It was a different story at Hale's office. Hale's once successful agency was now a sham. The phones seldom rang, and when they did, it was mostly curiosity seekers, reporters, or creditors worrying about getting paid.

Sylvia Mahoney had been on vacation in Hawaii when Hale's staff was originally questioned. She hadn't known about her boss's death until she returned, which was only yesterday.

She told Frank about a threat that Beck had made about a week before Everett and Cleo Hale had been murdered. She'd been alone in the office when Beck came storming in. Everyone else was either at lunch or out in the field.

"What was the nature of Beck's threat, Miss Mahoney?" Frank asked. "It would be helpful if you could remember as closely as possible his exact words."

"I don't know if I can quote him verbatim. It was, after all, a few weeks ago." She frowned. "I just wish I'd known that Mr. Hale had been murdered sooner." Her tone was accusatory. "I left a number. Someone should have called me."

"Beck's threat?" Frank prompted.

"Yes, of course. It was about Miramba. He said something about breaking Mr. Hale's contract with her the same way Mr. Hale had done it to him. That it would be messy. That Mr. Hale would be sorry." The woman had a smug look on her face when she added, "He also said that if Mr. Hale held Miramba to her contract, he'd find another way to get him out of her life. If that isn't a threat, I don't know what is." She sniffed. "Mr. Beck was very angry. For a moment I thought he might hit me. As it was, he slammed his fist down on my desk. He broke a paper weight." Resentment filled her voice. "It was a gift from a dear friend."

Warrants were obtained to search Beck's office and apartment in cooperation with the Burbank police department. Allandro was with Beck on both searches. Buried under a pile of socks were letters from several women, many of them strangers to Frank. Two sets of letters grabbed him. One set was from Miramba, hot and steamy messages with sexual inferences. It was the stack of letters from Cleo Hale that made his heart beat faster. They dated back to the days before she'd married Everett Hale. It was the last one, postmarked only a few days before the Hale killings, that Frank concentrated on. One paragraph in particular leaped out at him. "I can't stay with him much longer. I should have never married him. I have to see you. We're going to the beach house this weekend. I can sneak away from him. Call me."

The need to place Beck on the scene was of paramount importance now.

Frank and Tom split the beach colony in half, each armed with a picture of Doug Beck. Tom took Sarah Meadows under protest.

"She trusts you, Tom," Frank urged.

Later they compared notes. No one had seen Doug Beck at the colony the night of the Hale killings. Only one of the residents said they'd ever seen him at any time. Sarah Meadows. She'd seen him with Cleo, Tom said.

"She wasn't sure at first, Frank. She said she only caught a glimpse of him when he stepped out on the patio of the Hale beach house with Mrs. Hale. But that's nothing we didn't already suspect. We figured he was the one who came to the colony with Cleo Hale. It's what she and Everett Hale argued about, remember? She didn't see him that night." Tom grinned. "If she had of, she'd have shouted it from the rooftops. She's one nosy broad."

Frank sighed. "I was afraid of that. If we can't put him on or near the scene, all we have is Sheila Beck's statement, Cleo's vague invitation, and a lot of circumstantial evidence."

"Will the D.A. go with what we've got?"

Frank shook his head. "I don't know. There's still Cleo's six-carat diamond. I wish we could have found it in Beck's possession. Or at least evidence that he had it and disposed of it."

"You don't seem very optimistic."

"I'm not. Ever since Sheila Beck walked into the Burbank station, it's been like a scavenger hunt with a convenient trail of items strewn along the way, with someone holding back the final item that's needed to win the hunt."

"Another one of your famous hunches, Frank?"

Frank gave him a long hard stare in answer.

It was the first time since they'd teamed up that Frank had shut him out. Tom pretended it didn't bother him. "Now what?"

"We bring him in."

***

Right before Allandro booked Beck in Burbank, another unexpected breakthrough occurred.

A highway patrolman reading about the developments in the Hale case in his local newspaper where Beck's name was being freely tossed around, remembered giving him a ticket. A check of his records revealed that the ticket had been issued for speeding the night the Hales were murdered. The time was 11:17 p.m. The location, Thousand Oaks.

After Allandro booked Beck for suspicion of murder, he was released into Frank's custody for transportation to Santa Barbara where he was to be interrogated. Frank sat across the table from Beck. Beck's attorney was present. His name was Edward Schmidt. Schmidt was a high powered criminal attorney, and he was expensive. Frank couldn't help wondering where Beck was going to get the money to pay him.

"Make it easy on yourself, Beck," Frank began. "Don't take the fall alone. You weren't by yourself the night Everett and Cleo Hale were killed. Who was with you?"

"About three hundred people. I was at a party, remember?"

"Penny Downing says you left about ten. And that you were sober. That doesn't match the story you gave me."

"Sure it does. Who the hell is Penny Downing? So I didn't tell you everything. I left the party for a while. I drove around. I started back home, then realized there was no one waiting for me there, so I turned around and went back to the party. Someone slipped something in my drink. Everything after that is exactly the way I told you it was."

"How far did you drive after you left the party?"

"I don't know. A ways."

"Thousand Oaks?"

Beck glanced at his attorney. He placed a hand over Schmidt's ear and whispered something. Schmidt whispered something back.

"Could be," Beck answered.

"Let me refresh your memory," Frank said. "On your way to the beach house you were stopped by a highway patrolman. You received a ticket for speeding."

"So, I got a ticket. I suppose you don't get any. Cop's privilege?"

Frank ignored the challenge. "Thousand Oaks is a long way from Beverly Hills."

"It's also a long way from the beach house."

"About the same difference. Around sixty miles. You said you just drove around. Do you make a habit of taking aimless sixty mile drives?"

"I've been known to. I was distracted. It had been a rough day."

Frank changed his line of questioning.

"Your wife says you weren't home at four-thirty in the morning. She was at your apartment."

"I already said I wasn't sure what time I got home. It could have been after four-thirty."

"Not according to you. You said there was an old Barbara Stanwyk movie on television. We checked. The movie started at one-thirty. It ended at three-thirty."

"Maybe it was another movie. All those old black and while movies look the same after a while."

"Nice try. The only part of your story that checks is leaving the television on for your dog. Your wife verified that minor detail."

"She also told you I said I killed Everett and Cleo. What kind of an idiot confesses murder to his estranged wife?"

Frank had to admit it was their one weak link. "You're saying she's lying?"

"Of course she is."

"Why?"

"Revenge. She wanted us to get back together. I didn't want any part of a reconciliation."

"I'm not buying it, Beck. She doesn't seem like the type."

"To want to get back together?"

"To want to get even."

Beck reached for a cigarette. He lighted it and blew smoke in Frank's face. "How the hell would you know? You don't know anything about her. Or about me."

"I think you had a hand in killing Everett and Cleo Hale. Who was with you, Beck?" Frank urged.

"Go fuck yourself, Damien. No one was with me at the Hale beach house. No one. Because I wasn't there. You can't prove I was."

"We don't have to. We have your wife."

Beck threw back his head and laughed. "Then you have nothing."

For just a moment, Beck's arrogance and his air of self assurance was like stepping back in time. To that awful day in Cordova's office when Frank had realized Cordova was The Artist and that he'd been played like a cat with a mouse.

Schmidt intervened. "I've been very patient with you, Damien, because my client wanted to tell his side of the story. Against my advice I might add. Now I feel compelled to step in." He gave Beck a warning glance.

"Any conversations my client had with his wife are confidential. I'm sure I don't need to remind you that a wife can't be made to testify against her husband."

"We don't need her testimony, Mr. Schmidt. Sheila Beck was only the catalyst that led us to Beck. We have a strong enough case without her. We have Cleo's last letter to your client, Penny Downing's statement that refutes Beck's own account of his whereabouts, and we have the speeding ticket in Thousand Oaks that places him sixty miles away from where he claimed to be."

"All of which adds up to nothing more than circumstantial evidence," Schmidt retorted.

"Fuck it," Beck exploded. "Let the bitch testify, Ed. She's lying, and we can prove it."

Schmidt angrily turned on his client. "Shut up, Doug. Either that or get yourself another attorney. I was hired to defend you. I can't do that if you insist on practicing law all by yourself." He turned his attention back to Frank. "I repeat, Detective Damien, Shelia Beck will not testify against her husband."

Frank stared intently at Beck. What was the matter with the son of a bitch? He was acting like he wanted to go to trial. He experienced a familiar pang of uneasiness. He motioned to the guard at the door. "I'm finished with him for now. Let me out of here."

He looked back over his shoulder at Beck. "I don't know what your game is Beck...yet, but I intend to find out. If you're protecting someone, we'll find him. Or her," he added thoughtfully.

***

The charges of murder against Simkins and Manderell were dropped. They were charged instead, with a misdemeanor, and fined for their failure to report the discovery of the Hale jewelry. When they couldn't pay the fine, they were given thirty days with credit for time served.

Doug Beck was released.

Frank argued with the D.A., Bart Crossman. "You can't just let him go. He's guilty." Frank placed a hand across his heart. "I feel it...here."

Crossman slapped the lid closed on his briefcase. "Feeling is one thing. Evidence is another. Can you give me enough evidence to prove it, Damien?"

"What about the letter from Cleo, the ticket, his lying about what time he left the party?"

"Circumstantial. If that's all you're got, he'll walk. Is that what you want?"

"You know I don't."

"Then build a case I can use. Then, I'll prosecute."

It was a bitter pill to swallow, but Frank had no choice but to retreat.

***

A week later the Rowland boy died without ever regaining consciousness. There was growing concern that the same person who'd killed Everett and Cleo Hale and possibly the Rowlands would kill again. Frank found himself in the minority when he insisted the murders weren't connected.

It was the same week Frank found out that Miramba was paying Beck's attorney. And from Tom he learned that Derek Hale was still missing.

CHAPTER 7

Frank was suffering from a bad case of the guilts for the way he'd treated Marian the day she'd called about Derek's disappearance. He called her to tell her he was on his way over to see her.

It had been over an hour since Frank had called. Marian Hale couldn't stop fidgeting. She couldn't help asking herself why was Frank coming over? What if he sent someone else at the last minute? If he did, would it matter? She knew it would.

The first thing Frank noticed when he drove up to the house was the SOLD sign on the lawn.

When the doorbell rang, Marian started. She forced herself to walk to the front door instead of obeying the natural urge to run.

When she opened the door, her first thought was that Frank looked tired, preoccupied, and wary.

"Come in, Frank. I mean, Detective Damien. I've been on edge ever since you called. Is it about Derek?"

He liked the sound of his name on her lips. "Call me Frank. If you don't mind, I'll call you Marian."

She flushed. "I don't mind at all."

She steered him to the living room. "Can I get you something? Coffee? Beer?"

"Nothing, thanks." He took a seat. "I checked with Missing Persons. There's nothing new on Derek."

She plopped herself wearily down in a chair opposite him. "Thank God! I thought you'd come here to tell me he was dead." She leaned forward. "Where can he be? I'm so afraid for him."

He cursed his thoughtlessness. He should have told her right away that no news was good news at this point. He also knew he owed it to her to prepare her for the worst. "I'm sorry about the other day. I was insensitive. I should have come myself instead of sending someone else."

"Well, you're here now."

She was making it easier for him. He silently thanked her. "There's things you ought to know. When someone has been gone as long as Derek has, especially a juvenile, without some kind of communication, it usually means one of several things."

She leaned closer.

"Either he ran away and doesn't want to be found, he was coerced, and isn't free to communicate, or," he hesitated, "there's been foul play."

She paled. "Don't think I haven't thought about that. I wake in the middle of the night in a cold sweat thinking about it. It's the not knowing that's killing me."

"I know how you feel. Did Derek have a reason to run away?"

Everything was going so well, he was taken back by her sudden change of attitude. "You can't possibly know how I feel. And no, there's no reason for Derek to have run off." She turned on him angrily. "You're thinking his disappearance has something to do with Ev's death."

"Didn't you? It took you a while to report him missing. Until we brought in Simkins and Manderell as a matter of fact."

"I don't like the implication."

"At the time, neither did I."

Frank sighed. Now was as good a time as any to tell her about Beck. He hit the highlights about Sheila Beck's surprise statement and Beck's arrest. "News of his arrest and release will be in all the papers tonight. The D.A. doesn't think we have enough on him to win a case. I know he did it, and I'm going to prove it."

"That puts Derek in the clear! It means he didn't do it."

He stared at her in stunned silence. Poor Marian. All this time she'd believed her son had killed his father. "No. He didn't, but he could have seen something at the beach house that morning he didn't tell me about, or anyone else."

Her face turned ashen. "Are you saying he's in danger? That someone might want to hurt him? But you just said that Doug…"

He responded to her distress. "Don't get upset. I'm simply thinking out loud." He stood and moved closer to her. He placed his hands on her shoulders and quickly withdrew them. "Derek must have visited your ex-husband more than a few times. Is it possible he knew Doug Beck?"

"I don't think so. I told you Ev and Doug Beck weren't friends, so Derek could have hardly met him on a social level, and Ev didn't like the kids to go by his office. So your really think Doug Beck killed Ev and Cleo?"

"I think he's guilty as hell."

"In spite of the fact that another couple were beaten to death in San Diego?"

"Different MO's. My guess is that the San Diego murders were done by a copycat killer. Brutal or bizarre killings bring them crawling out of the woodwork like worms."

"MO's?"

"Modus operandi. The method of procedure. It works like a fingerprint in a lot of ways."

She sighed. "Then it's over."

"Not until I can put Beck away, it isn't. Can you think of anything that will help me?"

She shook her head. "God knows I'd like to."

She looked so defenseless, Frank wanted to sweep her into his arms. But he didn't. "I'd better be going. I'll try to get them to put extra manpower on Derek's disappearance. Don't get your hopes up. Kids drop out of sight every day. Some of them never surface. You have to prepare yourself for that."

"I have, thanks to you."

He pulled on his ear lobe. "Well, I'd better get to it."

She tilted her head to one side. "You're always running away from me. Just what are you afraid of? Who or what is it you see when you look at me that scares you off?"

"Where the hell did that come from?"

"It's true, isn't it? It might help to talk about it."

He shrugged. It would almost be a relief to tell her. "In a lot of ways you remind me of my wife, Claire."

"And that's bad?"

"It could be."

"Is she dead?"

"She might just as well be."

"That's very cryptic."

He ignored the challenge to respond. He made an effort to be flip. "Sorry, we'll have to continue this walk back into my past some other time. I really do have to go. If you hear from your son, call me."

"I will. I sold the house, by the way. Escrow closes in a month. What do I do if Derek hasn't come home by then? He won't know where to find me."

Frank's heart skipped a beat. "You're leaving the area?"

"Why, Frank! I think you'd be upset if I did!"

It struck him just how upset he'd be. He wanted her more now than he did the first time he'd been here, but he couldn't let her see that. "Sure I'd be upset. I'm in the middle of an investigation of which you're a part."

He hadn't fooled her. She smiled. "I'm not leaving Santa Barbara. But it's nice to know you care." She surprised him by reaching over and planting a kiss on his cheek. "Thanks for coming." She smiled. "And thanks for calling me Marian and letting me call you Frank. I've a feeling it means a lot." He didn't answer her. Instead, he strode toward his car. He was two blocks away when he tenderly rubbed the spot where Marian had kissed him.

It was the next day. Frank looked up from a stack of paperwork when Tom placed his hand on his shoulder. "They found a body floating in the surf this morning."

"Has anyone called Marian Hale yet?"

"I don't think so. I guess it's up to Missing Persons."

"Have they been notified?"

"I don't know."

Frank's hand moved to his phone. "Who's in charge over there?"

"Bezinski. Jerry Bezinski."

Frank picked up the receiver, dialed a number and asked for Bezinski. When he came on the line, Frank said, "This is Frank Damien. I'm working the Hale murder case. The body on the beach this morning? I understand there's a possibility it could be the Hale kid."

Frank heard paper shuffling. "Derek Hale?"

"Yeah. Do me a favor, Bezinski. Let me take a look at the body first. I met the kid. I can give a tentative ID. If it's not the Hale boy, no sense in putting Marian Hale through the ordeal. If it is…well, she can always come down and give you a positive ID later."

A long sigh traveled the wire. Missing Persons was a thankless job filled with long tedious trails that usually ended nowhere. Sometimes like now the trail ended at the County Morgue. "Be my guest. You'll let me know?"

"Sure."

Frank looked up at Tom. "You want to go with me?"

"Okay." He hesitated. "It's none of my business, Frank, but about Marian Hale? Is there…?"

Frank grabbed his jacket from the back of his chair. He stood. "You're right, Tom, it's none of your business."

Down at the morgue, a white-coated attendant pulled out a drawer containing the John Doe found on the beach. His motions were mechanical as he pulled back the sheet to expose a badly bloated body. There were chunks of flesh missing. Something, a small shark possibly, had desecrated the human flesh.

Frank stared down at what had once been a living thing. Somebody would have reason to grieve the loss of this poor bastard, dead before he'd had a chance to experience life.

It wouldn't be Marian Hale.

Frank instructed the attendant to close the drawer.

When he arrived back at his office, he immediately called Bezinski. "The John Doe at the morgue is still a John Doe. It's not Derek Hale."

There was a familiar sigh in response. "Of course it isn't. That would have been too fucking easy."

***

Frank waited for Marian Hale to answer his knock. He'd made up his mind to quit fighting his attraction to her. To hell with the fact that it wasn't smart to mess around with anyone involved, however innocently, with a murder case. To hell with the fact that she reminded him of Claire. Claire was lost to him. It was time he faced that reality, he told himself. Time to start living again. Time to allow himself to feel again.

There was an uneasy smile on Marian's face when she answered the door. "Derek?" she asked.

"No. Not exactly. Can I come in?"

She opened the door wider. "Sorry. Of course you can."

Frank followed her into the living room. "Is your daughter around?"

"Yes, she's upstairs. Why?"

"She may know something about Derek's disappearance, Marian. Kids have a way of covering for each other. How close are you to Joanna?"

"Close enough to know she wouldn't hide anything from me. That is what you're implying, isn't it?

"Don't be so damned defensive. I'm not implying anything. I'm trying to find out what happened to your son. At the Beach house, the morning he found his father and Cleo dead, he hinted that he knew something. When I came here the next day, he was subdued. I still think it's possible he saw something, or heard something. If he didn't tell me or you, he might have told his sister."

Marian shook her head vigorously. "He was grandstanding at the beach house that day."

"Then what harm will it do to talk to Joanna?"

Marian was close to tears. "I had two children, Frank. Now I only have one. I've faced the fact that Derek may not be alive. You made me do that. At first I hated you for it. Now, I see you were only trying to help me. Joanna has been through a lot. I don't want her subjected to an interrogation."

Frank threw up his hands. "Jesus Christ, Marian. Look around you. Did I bring an army? I don't want to interrogate her, I just want to ask her a few simple questions."

She looked unsure. "All right. I'll fetch her. And, Frank?"

"Yes?"

"Be gentle."

Joanna didn't seem nearly as concerned as her mother about Frank wanting to talk to her again. In response to Frank's question, "Did Derek tell you he was leaving?" she answered "No. But then Derek and I didn't confide in each other. We weren't close. Derek was an intellectual. I'm an air head in comparison."

"Joanna," Marian said sharply. "Don't talk about Derek in the past tense."

"Why not?" She chimed in on her mother. "You've been acting like he's dead."

Frank intervened. "What do YOU think, Joanna? Do you think he's dead?"

She shrugged. "I don't know what to think. He can be a pain in the ass, but he is my brother, and I love him, and I want him to come home. I don't know where he is, or why he left."

"Did the two of you discuss your father's murder?"

"At first. Then we stopped talking about it. It was easier for both of us that way."

"Did he tell you anything he might not have discussed with anyone else?"

"Like what?"

It was a fair question, Frank allowed. What in the hell did he expect to find out? "You and your brother visited your father?"

"Yes."

"Did you or he ever meet Doug Beck?"

"The man you think killed my father and Cleo?" She smiled. "Mother told me. I don't think so. I know I never met him."

"I told you that Ev and Doug weren't on a social basis," Marian intervened, "and that Ev had a thing about the children going to his office."

Frank looked over at Joanna.

"It's true. Daddy was a brute about it."

"I think that's enough," Marian interjected. "She can't tell you what she doesn't know. You can go back to your room now, Joanna."

After Joanna left the room, Frank said, "I wasn't going to bite her."

"I know. It's just that...there's been so much to handle. I hate not knowing where Derek is."

"I'll try to find him, Marian."

"Why?" She accused. "Because you think he's the key to your investigation?"

I miss Claire so much at times like this, Frank thought. She allowed me to think out loud. To put my thoughts in order. "I want us to be friends, Marian."

"Just friends?"

She was pushing. Despite his earlier self-counseling Frank wasn't sure he was really ready for a relationship. Or, if in fact that was what Marian was offering him.

"You must have loved your wife very much," she said. You said I reminded you of her. I'm not sure that's healthy. I don't want to walk in someone else's shadow. I think you'd better leave."

"What if I don't want to?"

"You don't?"

"No."

"Then what do we talk about? I'm tired of talking about Ev's death, and even more tired of thinking about it. I'm sick of worrying about Derek so I don't want to talk about him either. I suspect you're not ready to talk about your wife, or discuss what went wrong between the two of you."

"Who said we have to talk?"

The air was pregnant with unspoken words. Filled with tension and untended passion.

They stood, facing one another, neither making a move toward the other. It was Frank who finally made an overture. He stepped so close to her she could feel the heat of his breath. He placed his hands on her shoulders, then slowly drew her to him.

His kiss was searching, hesitant. She would never believe, he thought, that I haven't held a woman in my arms, or wanted to, since Claire left me. When he felt her warm response, he was heartened, encouraged to give his kiss more meaning.

She suddenly pulled away from him.

"What's the matter?" he asked.

"I'm not sure this is right for either of us. There are things about you that frighten me, Frank. You're so intense."

"Are you asking me to leave?"

"Yes. No. I don't know. Maybe you'd better go." Her glance strayed toward the staircase. "Besides, Joanna is upstairs."

Frank pulled his notebook out of his jacket. He tore off a page and jotted down his address and phone number. "I won't press you. Anyway, believe it or not, I'm just as afraid as you are of what I'm feeling." He handed her the piece of paper. "If you want to see me, call me. If you don't, I'll understand."

She palmed the piece of paper with his address on it. "You're a good man, Frank Damien. Maybe that's what really scares me."

Despite the tension, Frank couldn't resist laughing. "Look at us! We're acting like teenagers, yet we're both past the age of consent. I'm thirty-eight, scared, afraid to take a risk, and at the same time afraid of growing old alone. And, you? I can only guess. Your husband was no saint. I don't know what you had with him, or how much you really cared. I only know how much I'm beginning to care about you."

Before she could respond, he swiftly left. I've made my move, he thought, as he drove away from the house. Whatever happens next, or doesn't happen, is up to her.

***

Frank flipped on the television. I really must buy a bigger TV, he promised himself. He changed channels three times. He couldn't get interested in any one program.

It's that woman, he inwardly cursed. He walked to the phone, picked it up, pushed three buttons then hung up. He picked the instrument back up. This time he dialed the whole number. It rang once before he hung up. He was staring at the receiver trying to make up his mind whether he should complete the call to Marian when the door bell rang.

He checked the clock on the wall. It was after eleven. Who in the hell would come here this time of night? Probably Tom.

He opened the door. Marian Hale stood there. She smiled. "Tell me about Claire."

CHAPTER 8

Once he began, it was easier than Frank had ever thought possible to talk about Claire. After the first few minutes, he couldn't seem to stop. He told Marian how they'd met, and how Claire had captured his heart in those first few minutes.

"I thought I was the luckiest man alive," he said. "I was brought up in a tough neighborhood. When I was a kid my mother used to shake her head at my brother and me. She'd wag her finger and say, "You boys. You got choices. There are two sides to the law. In this neighborhood you either are the law, or you're bucking it. I still can remember the look of pride on my mother's face when she watched me graduate from the academy."

"And your brother?" Marian asked.

Frank had been sitting beside her on the couch that needed recovering. He walked to the kitchen, took two beers from the refrigerator, and when she shook her head, put one back. He popped the top of the can. "He made a different choice. They found him in an alley one night. They said it was an accidental overdose, but I knew differently. He was dealing. He crossed his suppliers. They killed him."

"I'm so sorry."

He shrugged. "It was a long time ago."

"You said you felt lucky?"

"I did. Claire was like a flower in a garden full of weeds. Gentle and yet strong. Genteel but not snobbish. I never expected to find anyone like her. Not with my background. And not with my job. You have to remember, pimps, prostitutes, and junkies were my daily diet."

"How long before you were married?"

"Six months. I would have married her that first day." He smiled. "It took me that long to get up the courage to ask her."

"How long were you married?"

"Five years."

"Children?"

"No. Claire wanted them. I couldn't seem to reconcile myself to bringing a child into this lousy screwed up world. Later, about three years after we were married, I gave in because she wanted kids so badly. It didn't happen for us. Claire went to see a doctor about a year before we split up. She came out with a clean bill of health. She wanted me to take a fertility test. I put it off. Too goddamned macho, I guess. No man wants to think he can't reproduce.

"What happened between you and Claire?"

Frank drained the can of beer. He got up and reached into the refrigerator for another one. This time, Marian accepted one.

Frank felt his heart palpitating. Did he want to tell Marian everything? Did he want to relive the horror of it all. The helplessness.

Face it, he told himself. You've lived it every day since it happened. You go to bed with it at night, and you wake up with it in the morning.

He took a swallow of his beer. He told her about Cordova. About coming home and finding Claire sitting on the floor, covered with her own blood. About her suicide attempt and her depression.

"I can't get the picture of her sitting there like that out of my mind." His smile was grim. "Claire hated tears, and they streamed unchecked down her beautiful face." Funny, things that stick in your mind." A dark look passed across his face. I'd taken something good and let it get spoiled. There were cops all over the place violating her privacy. It was not unlike so many other crime scenes I'd attended, only now it was my home that was violated. My wife. My problem. It was then," he said, "that I realized I never should have married her. She was born for something better. When she was released from the sanitarium, I clung to the hope that we could put what Cordova did behind us. I only knew that the idea of life without her was unthinkable."

"She left you?"

"Yes. Me and my work. We were a constant reminder of what she'd been through. I offered to quit the force, but it was too late. The scars ran too deep."

Marian puller her feet under her and leaned back on the couch. "You still love her, don't you?"

"Maybe. I try not to think about it. She called me last year to tell me that she'd gotten married again, and that they were having a baby. She married an accountant." He laughed, the sound brittle. "Accountants don't encounter psychos or bring violence into their homes."

"And just maybe they don't love as deeply as you do. A woman is lucky to know that kind of love. Claire calling you like that out of the blue? That seems cruel. Out of character somehow for the picture of sainthood you just described."

"Did I do that? Claire's no saint." He grinned. "Damned close, though. And it wasn't so out of character. Claire knew how hard it was for me to adjust to life without her. Hell, I traveled all the way across the United States in order to put enough distance between us to cope with the pain of losing her. She realized how badly I needed to start living my own life. I think she was trying to cut the cord."

"I don't think she succeeded."

He pulled Marian to him. "Until recently I would have agreed with you. Then I met you."

She pulled away from him. "I won't be a clone for Claire."

"I don't want you to be. I said you reminded me of her. There are differences. Sharp differences. I want to be with you. Beyond that I can't promise you anything."

Distrust filled her eyes. "I don't know, Frank. Instinct tells me not to get involved with you."

"Then why did you come here? It couldn't have been just curiosity."

She stood, folded her arms across her chest and said, "Damn you."

He rose and pulled her to him. His lips brushed her neck, her cheek, and found her mouth. Their lips met. "I want you, Marian," he whispered. "If you think you can't handle that, then leave."

Instead of answering him, she clung to him. When he led her to the bedroom, she didn't resist. He laid her gently down on the bed.

Frank slowly undressed her. His heart beat wildly. How long since he'd done this? Four years? More than that. It was a long time to have gone without love, physical or otherwise. For one wild moment he was reminded of the first time he'd taken a girl's virginity, the same night he'd given up his own. He'd been scared then. He was scared now.

When Marian was naked, he stared in wonder. He was going to make love to this woman, and she was going to make love to him. He shed his own clothes, glad that he worked out and his body was still trim. He lowered himself down beside her and took her shyly into his arms. Their lips met in an urgent kiss. His fingers caressed her breasts and found her softness. She, in turn sought and found his sex and moved her fingers in vertical motions. He sucked in his breath. Her touch set fire to his skin. Emboldened by her own moves, his lips traveled downward, stopping short of the prize he sought to claim. She encouraged him with a slight movement of her hand. Then, incredibly, while his mouth claimed her, hers found him. He felt like he was going to explode. Afraid he couldn't control his need to be inside her a moment longer, he penetrated her, his thrusts causing her to rake her nails down his back, but he felt no pain, only intense pleasure. Her soft moans harmonized with his own.

Their breathing heavy, they lay in quiet reflection afterwards. It occurred to Frank that Marian was more prepared for what had happened than he. Then, by her own admission she'd had an affair not too long ago. He wondered who the lucky bastard was, and why he'd let her get away from him. Marian broke the silence. "I've been so very wrong about you."

"Really? Like how?"

She sighed. "It's not important now. Where do we go from here, Frank?"

He sat up in bed, reached for a cigarette, lighted it, and said, "You've had a glimpse of my life. Are you sure you want to be a part of it?"

"Are you asking me to be?"

"Yes. I'd be lying if I said I was looking for something permanent, lying if I said I wasn't. I don't know what I want. I offered to quit the force for Claire. She knew I couldn't do it, knew there will always be a case like Cordova and the murders of Everett and Cleo Hale, and that I'll never rest until I solve them and can put whoever commits such senseless acts away. That's why I have to get more on Beck and whoever he's protecting."

"Protecting?"

"He wasn't alone at the beach house. I'd stake my life on it."

She frowned. "I don't understand. Are you saying now that you don't think Beck killed Ev and Cleo?"

She took him off guard by pulling away from him. She slid her feet to the floor and reached for her clothes. "Sorry, Frank. You can't sleep with me then shut me out. I'm not asking you to divulge state secrets or even departmental ones. I just want you to trust me. I had that bond with Ev once, and I'm betting you had it with Claire. I won't settle for less. Not with you, nor with anyone else."

Frank slipped into his pants. "You ask a hell of a lot."

"You mean for a casual lay?" she flared.

"You know it isn't like that."

"Then why does it suddenly feel like it?"

Marian retrieved her purse from the coffee table in the living room. "It took a lot for me to come here tonight. It's going to take a lot more to bring me back."

Frank watched her leave, a feeling of helplessness washing over him. He knew that until he was willing to offer her more than a piece of himself, he had no right to stop her.

***

Frank and Marian were managing an uneasy truce. He asked her to dinner. She accepted. When he dropped her off at home after the meal and left after only a hesitant kiss, she was angry.

When he invited her to see a play a few days later, she coldly accepted with the admonition, "Is this to be a replay of the other night?"

When he didn't answer, she said, "Just so long as I know the ground rules."

It was the same night that she told him about the phone call. "There was someone on the other end of the line, Frank. I swear it was Derek, but he wouldn't say anything. What does it mean?"

He'd shrugged. "If you're right, if it was Derek, it means he's alive. That's something to be grateful for. Maybe he wants to come home."

"Then why doesn't he? Why call and refuse to talk to me?"

"I can't answer that."

She threw him a look of sheer exasperation. "What are your people doing about his disappearance? I haven't heard a word from Missing Persons lately, and damned little from you."

"What do you want from us, Marian? From me? One missing kid can't become a department priority."

"You said you'd make it yours."

"I can't, Marian. That isn't what I said, anyway. You're being unreasonable. You know my priority right now has to be Beck."

"I don't know any such thing. Talk to me, Frank. Tell me what you think happened at the beach house."

She was asking him once again for his trust. It wasn't a matter of trust, but of getting his thoughts in order. How was he going to convince her of that?

"All I have is mere conjecture at this point."

"I'll settle for that."

"All right. I've always believed that there were two people there that night. That whoever killed them didn't do it alone. Lately, I've adjusted that theory." There was excitement in his voice. "Consider this. What if Beck went to the beach house to kill Everett Hale? That it was a premeditated act, planned by him and Cleo."

She frowned. "I don't follow you. Cleo was killed that night."

"I admit my theory has a hell of a lot of wrinkles. After Everett Hale was murdered Beck could have panicked, realized that Cleo was the only one who could send him to the gas chamber. From all I've learned about her, she was a temperamental bitch, ambitious enough to crush anyone who stood in her way, and probably capable of blackmail if it suited her purpose. Beck may have figured that killing her was his only insurance. Speaking of insurance, there's that million dollar policy your ex-husband took out on himself with Cleo as his beneficiary."

"That was a surprise, and a boon for the children, but it makes no sense, Frank. If he killed Everett to have Cleo and the money, what would killing her accomplish?"

Frank shook his head. "I don't know. This whole goddamned case has holes in it. Anyway, I said it was only a theory."

"You really don't think that Beck was at the beach house by himself?"

"No, I don't."

"You seem so sure of that."

"It's the one thing I am sure of."

It wasn't until after he once again left her with only a goodnight kiss that he realized that he'd been able to think out loud in the presence of someone again, and he had to admit it had felt good.

***

His sense of well-being was shattered two days later when a report came in that a boy answered to Derek's description had tried to hock a diamond ring in a San Francisco pawn shop.

The pawnbroker had managed to hold onto the ring, but the boy had gotten away. It was Cleo Hale's six-carat diamond.

It had been three weeks since Doug Beck had been released from custody. Frank waited in Beck's outer office. Beck's receptionist, after deliberately ignoring him, finally told him he could go on into Beck's inner office.

Beck offered him a chair. Frank refused it. "What I came here to say won't take long."

Beck insolently leaned back in his oversized leather desk chair. Like everything else in the room it was a new expensive.

"Just what is it that brought you here, Damien?"

Frank looked around the room. "New furnishings?" he asked.

"Yeah. So what?"

"Business must be good. Ah, but then you have a benefactor now. Miramba. Just how much did she shell out to Schmidt on your behalf?"

Beck pulled himself up out of the chair. "You didn't come here to discuss the fucking furniture or Schmidt's fee. Get to the point."

"You played a good game, Beck. Damn good, I grant you. I'm curious? How in the hell did you get your wife to put on such a good act? Turning you in was an act of genius. Of course, she could have a good reason for doing it, like she could have helped you to kill the Hales. Or then again, she could just be an innocent pawn whose feelings for you, you used to your own advantage."

"You have your nerve, Damien. I was released, remember?"

"But not exonerated. Far from it. If I can find the man or woman who was with you at the beach house that night, it's a new ball game."

Doug Beck looked worried for the first time since Frank had entered the room.

"You're full of crap, Damien."

"Maybe, but suddenly you're not so sure, are you? Allow me the luxury of thinking out loud for a moment. You could have planned to kill Hale with Cleo's help, then killed her to protect yourself. Am I getting close, Beck?"

Beads of sweat appeared on Beck's forehead. "What you ARE doing is making me fucking angry. I don't have to sit here and take this." Beck pressed the intercom buzzer. "Debbie. Get me police headquarters."

"Turning yourself in, Beck?"

"Cute. I was thinking of turning you in. I don't appreciate being harassed."

Frank smiled. "You can cancel that call. I'm on my way out." He looked back over his shoulder and added. "I don't suppose you know anything about Derek Hale's disappearance, or how he got a hold of Cleo's ring?"

Beck's facial muscles tightened. "The kid has Cleo's ring! That little son of a bitch! He probably stole it."

"Maybe. Or maybe someone gave it to him."

"You think I gave it to him? Why? I didn't kill Cleo, Damien. I loved her. And I sure as hell didn't give a six-carat diamond ring to Hale's kid. Maybe you should ask his mother where he got it."

That, Frank thought, was on his list of things to do, and he wasn't looking forward to it.

***

From Beck's office, Frank made his way across town to Beck's apartment. Sheila Beck answered the door.

Consternation filled her face. "Doug isn't home."

"I didn't come here to see your husband. It was you I came to see."

Her wariness increased. "Why?"

"For openers, what are you doing here in Beck's apartment? I thought you and he were separated."

"We were. We are. I've sent for Kevin. Doug has been wonderful since his arrest. He wants me and Kevin with him. It's not a reconciliation, not yet, anyway, but it's a start. Doug needs me now."

Frank shook his head. "Is that what your husband wants you to believe? Or what you want me to believe? What are you, Mrs. Beck? A consummate liar or an incredible actress?"

She frowned. "I don't understand."

"I think you do. What did Beck do or say to make you turn him in for murdering Everett and Cleo Hale? What kind of hold does he have on you? Did you go into this thing with your eyes wide open, or were you duped? Then there's Miramba? What's her role? Is she trying to take her sister's place in your husband's life?"

She nervously looked at the clock in the wall. Almost six. Beck would be home soon. "That's a really rotten thing to say. Miramba means nothing to Doug."

Frank thought about the letters he'd found in Beck's apartment. He was sure Sheila knew about them. He sighed. He handed her his business card. "Forget it, Mrs. Beck, if you change your mind and would like to talk to me, about anything, anything at all , call me."

***

Waiting for Marian to answer the door, Frank thought about what he was going to say to her. No matter how he phrased it, telling her about Derek wasn't going to be easy.

"You look awful," she said. "Come in. What's the matter?"

He took her arm and led her into the living room. He sat her down on a chair. "It's Derek," he said.

"Is he…?"

"No, but he's been seen."

"Thank God," Then, "What is it, Frank?"

"Someone, who we're sure was Derek, tried to pawn Cleo's ring in San Francisco."

She turned so pale Frank thought she was going to pass out. "Cleo's ring? That's impossible. What would he be doing with Cleo's ring?"

"I was hoping you could tell me."

"No. I can't, because I don't know how he got it, or even if he had it at all. How do you know it was Derek? It could have been someone who looked like him."

"It's not likely. They faxed us a copy of a police sketch done with the help of the pawnbroker." Frank reached inside his jacket and pulled out a manila envelope. He extracted an 8 x 11 piece of paper with the police sketch on it. It looked exactly as he remembered Derek. He showed it to her.

She clapped her hand over her mouth. "Oh, my God."

He placed his arm on her shoulder, forcing her to look at him. "Marian, if you're holding something back, it isn't smart. I can't help you, if you won't help me."

She ripped the police sketch in half. "There's nothing I can say to help you. Now, please, just leave me alone."

***

Cliff Markham banged his fist down on his battle-scarred desktop. "God dammit, Frank. If you don't quit harassing Beck and his wife, you're looking at a suspension, sure as hell. Beck is screaming like a banshee. He wants your ass. For your sake, and for the sake of the case we hope to build against him, take it easy."

"You're right, Cliff. Sorry. Patience never was one of my virtues."

"Try to be patient. If he's guilty, we'll get him."

Markham began to sift through a pile of paperwork. When he looked up and saw that Frank hadn't left yet, he said, "Are you still here? Don't you have something to do? I know this isn't New York, but there must be some crime in this town that needs your attention. Other than the Hale case, I might add."

"I talked to Marian Hale today about her son and Cleo's ring. She took it hard."

Markham leaned back in his chair. He sighed. "You care about this woman, don't you?"

Frank flushed. "Is it all over the department?"

"No. It's my job to know what's going on with my men. Even if it were common knowledge, what the hell! What's important is what you feel. That's nobody's business but your own. We're cops, Frank, but we're also men. I don't think that being a cop should or does preclude us from having the same feelings as other men. Is it serious between you two?"

"It could get that way. That is, if we can get past what's going on with her son."

"Any more word on the boy?"

"No. He vanished again."

Markham shook his head. "It's a tough one, Frank, but if you care enough for each other, you'll find a way."

Maybe they would, and maybe they wouldn't, Frank thought. Then again, maybe it would be better if they didn't even try.

CHAPTER 9

The case against Beck was at a standstill. Despite a concentrated effort to prove otherwise, there was still no clear-cut evidence to place him at the scene of the Hale beach house the night of the Hale murders. Without that vital evidence, the D.A. wouldn't even consider re-opening the case. Frank found it intolerable.

Frank hadn't talked to Marian in over a week. Not since the day he'd told her about Derek and Cleo's ring.

She'd taken what was left after paying off debts from the house on the hill, and she'd purchased a three story older frame home close to downtown Santa Barbara, on Chapparral Street. She was opening an arts and crafts shop from the first floor of the house. She was starting life all over again from the bottom up. Frank admired her guts.

Meanwhile, a young transient, Darryl Cassady, who'd been arrested for attempted burglary in the Malibu area, confessed to the Rowland killings. Frank couldn't help feeling smug, he was denying that he had any part in the deaths of Everett and Cleo Hale.

Cassady had a history of violence and instability. He was Caucasian, seventeen, and a habitual offender. His crimes until now, at least the ones he'd been held accountable for, ranged from petty theft to aggravated assault. His record was a long one, dating back to when he was in grade school.

Coerced by his superiors to take part in an investigation to build a case against Cassady on the off chance he might very well have killed Everett and Cleo Hale, Frank once again joined forced with a fellow cop from another area. His name was John Mathias. Mathias was one of the many who thought that whoever killed the Rowlands had also killed the Hales.

He and Mathias conducted a search of Cassady's San Pedro waterfront rat infested two-room kitchen motel accommodations.

Frank inspected the suspect's bedroom, while Mathias concentrated on the tiny trash-filled living area. So far, Frank had found nothing, while Mathias had found damaging evidence in the form of parking tickets and receipts that proved Cassady had been in Santa Barbara and San Diego at the same time the bloody homicides had occurred at both locations. He also found press clippings of each of the murders.

"Look at this?" Mathias called out. "The Hale murders. What did I tell you?" His tone was triumphant. "Thank God we caught the son of a bitch before he killed anyone else. You know we think he was casing the house in Malibu that he broke into? That the owner of the house is a black entertainer with a live-in white female companion?"

Frank nodded. He'd heard all that. He still wasn't convinced.

Frank wandered into the living area, glanced at the Santa Barbara new Press clipping and shrugged. "It was Cassady's blueprint to kill the Rowlands. I still say he didn't kill Everett and Cleo Hale."

"What the fuck will it take to convince you? A confession?"

"Why not? He confessed to killing the Rowlands, and you can only go to the chair once."

A few minutes later Mathias found Frank sitting on Cassady's bed surrounded by pictures, booklets, and ticket stubs that Frank had found under a pile of clothes in an upper shelf in the bedroom closet. He was staring thoughtfully at the material when Mathias entered the room.

Mathias picked up one of the eight by ten glossies of Miramba. It was signed, "To Darryl, love Miramba." There were seven more pictures, all signed the same way. There were also booklets, the kind sold during a concert tour, and ticket stubs from major theaters across the state, including a ticket stub from the Universal Amphitheater the night Everett and Cleo Hale were killed.

"An avid fan," Mathias said. "Can't say I blame him. She's beautiful and she's talented. I tried to get tickets to one of her shows once. The only seats left were so far back it would have taken a telescope to see her. I passed." He pointed at the pictures, booklets, and ticket stubs and placed them in a box. "I don't know. It's probably a coincidence." Mathias snapped his fingers. "Of course! Miramba figured in the Hale murders, didn't she? Cleo Hale was Miramba's sister. You probably had her pegged as a suspect. Right?"

"For a while." Frank stood. "You finished in there? I'm through in here."

Mathias noted Frank's preoccupation. "What are you thinking, Frank? Are you thinking that Cleo Hale was killed by this son of a bitch because she was Miramba's sister? That his obvious obsession with Miramba started his killing spree?"

Frank shook his head. "Could be."

Mathias shrugged. "How come I don't believe that for one minute you believe that?"

Frank returned to Santa Barbara. He felt a restlessness born of frustration. Not a damn thing had been proved with Cassady's arrest. Nothing that had changed his mind about the Hale case being separate and apart from the Rowland murders or any other crime.

He longed for human contact.

He decided to test the waters with Marian.

It was fifteen minutes before seven when he called. Joanna answered the phone.

"Let me talk to your mother," Frank said.

"She's out." There was barely a moment's pause before she added. "With a man."

Frank's first thought was that Joanna Hale was enjoying this conversation. "Who's she with?"

"Nobody you know, Frank." He had a vivid picture of Joanna smiling as she added, "I can call you Frank, can't I? Detective Damien seems a trifle formal for someone who's sleeping with my mother, don't you think?"

At the silence on the other end of the line, she said, "Don't make the same mistake my mother did in thinking she could fool me. You have slept with her, haven't you?"

"I don't think that's any of your business."

"Really? Well, I don't see it that way. Especially when I've watched my mother spending days and nights waiting for you to call her. You never do any more. Why is that, Frank?"

"Didn't your mother tell you about Derek?"

"You mean the ring? If it really was Derek in San Francisco, then the little jackass stole it from the beach house before he called the police."

Maybe, Frank conceded. But why was that particular piece of jewelry left to steal? "Will you let your mother know I called?"

"I'll think about it."

The line went dead.

He was about to call back when his phone rang. A voice from the past, one he hadn't ever expected to hear again, was on the other end of the line. It was Captain Jenkins, his former New York Police Department superior officer. The sound of his voice created a wave of homesickness in Frank.

Jenkins was a man who came straight to the point. It was one of the things that Frank had always liked about him. "Cordova's dead, Frank."

Frank gripped the phone. Cordova dead! All he could think about was that he hoped he'd died slowly and horribly.

"Are you there, Frank?" Jenkins asked.

He was trembling. "Sure, Captain. I appreciate the call. How did he die?"

"He killed himself. He ground up glass and washed it down with water. It acted like a poison."

"Quick?"

Jenkins hesitated. He knew what Frank wanted to hear. "Yes, I'm sorry."

Not even a prolonged end! Where was the justice in that? "Thanks. Thanks for calling me, and thanks for not lying to me."

"I would never do that. I didn't just call to give you information, Frank. I need a favor."

"Ask it."

"It's Andy."

Frank's old partner had never gotten over his wife's death at Cordova's hands. He'd suffered a nervous breakdown that took him off the force. By the time Frank had left New York, Andy was for all intents and purposes, better. Acting almost normal again. "What about Andy?"

"When he learned about Cordova, instead of feeling satisfaction, he went to pieces again. I figured you'd understand why. He needs help,

Frank. You two were close. I was wondering if you would consider coming here to see him."

Because Frank had covered up his own near mental collapse, Jenkins had no way of knowing what he was asking of him. Frank knew exactly what Andy was going through. Andy's feeling like I am, he thought. Cheated out of our right to see justice done. "What can I possibly do for him, Captain? When he looks at me he sees a man whose wife survived. I saw that expression on his face when he was told Helen was dead and Claire was alive."

"You were his friend, Frank, and his partner. You lost your wife, too, in the end."

Jenkins was asking him to go back to New York. New York! Frank could almost smell it, feel the power of the city. It beckoned to him. But New York was Claire. And it had been Cordova. Could he go back there even just for a few days? Then again, could he not?

"Okay," Frank finally answered. "Where is he?"

"County hospital. Psychiatric ward."

"Bad?"

"Could be worse. I think it's just a relapse."

Frank swallowed. His voice when he spoke was uneven. "I'll be there."

Jenkins reacted to the distress in Frank's voice. "Hey, maybe this wasn't such a good idea. You have a new life now. How is it by the way?"

Frank thought about his earlier conversation with Joanna. " It's been okay, but right now, it sucks. Santa Barbara isn't New York, and never will be."

"I thought that was the whole idea, Frank."

"It was, and it is. I'll come to New York, but I can only stay a few days. I'm working a case here. A murder case."

"Good. Glad to see you're keeping your hand in. Want me to pick you up at the airport?"

"No, thanks. I'll catch a cab."

"You'll stop by to see me?"

"Sure." But neither of them believed that he would.

Instead of trying to call Marian again the next evening, Frank stopped by her new home. It was a far cry from the house on the hill, but its quiet unassuming elegance suited Marian. Joanna opened the door, gave him a knowing smile, and disappeared up the stairs.

Marian looked even lovelier than he'd remembered. He realized how much he'd missed her. He pointed to the stairs. "Your daughter thinks I'm playing with your affections."

Her silence was worse than any argument she might have made.

"Listen, Marian, we can't let Derek stand between us. I don't suppose you've heard from him?" No, of course not. You'd have called."

"Are you sure of that?"

"The truth? No, I'm not. Hell, it's your life, your son. I shouldn't have come here."

"Perhaps you shouldn't have. Tell me, Frank, do you want me? I mean not just in bed, but as a person?"

Frank sat down on the couch. "Yes, I do. But don't expect grandiose reasons. I don't have them."

She sat down beside him. "I was with a man last night. A friend. I slept with him, and it was awful for both of us. I wanted to find someone, anyone, to take your place in my thoughts. It didn't work. I can't say I like the idea of putting my future in your hands, but I don't seem to have a choice. You see, I want you, too."

He reached for her, but she stayed his outstretched arms. "There has to be ground rules, Frank. We both have pasts that are liable to get in the way of a successful relationship. Mine, seems to have been settled by fate. Ev is dead. Claire isn't."

How well he knew that. "I have to go back to New York for a few days."

She paled. "New York! Something to do with Claire?"

"No. It's my old partner. He's in trouble. I have to go see him."

"Then you won't be seeing Claire?"

"No."

She squared her shoulders. "I think you should, Frank. Sooner or later you have to put your ghosts to rest. If you can't do that, we don't have a prayer. Let me go with you," she pleaded. "I want to help you put the past behind you." Her face lit up. "We can make a vacation out of it."

Frank had been dreading going back to New York alone, so it wasn't hard to say yes to her. "You'd do that? You'd go with me?"

"Of course I would. I want us to be together, to build a future. She hesitated. "A future with marriage in it."

He frowned. "Then we have a problem. I'm not ready for marriage, Marian. It's all I can handle to be responsible for myself."

She gave him a sad smile. "I didn't mean right now. I'll wait. Not forever. But I'll wait. In the meantime, I'll sleep with you if that's what you want, but I won't live with you, or spend an entire night with you. To do that would be like giving into you and abandoning my principles. I have to hang onto them. It's all I have."

Frank had no basis for an argument. Not when he was offering her so little. He felt bad about it. "All right," he said. "We'll do it your way."

***

Frank stared out the porthole at the cluttered cloud cover. He glanced at his watch. Only an hour until they arrived at Kennedy Airport. He still couldn't believe he'd agreed to come to New York. It could only prove to be a painful journey down memory lane.

He glanced over at Marian. Her eyes were closed, although he suspected she wasn't asleep. How little we really know about each other, he reflected.

She opened her eyes. "What are you thinking?"

"I was wondering why in the hell I agreed to come. I must have been crazy. And, I was thinking that I know so little about you."

She smiled. "What do you want to know?"

"Everything."

"You mean my life before Ev?"

"That, too."

She leaned back in her seat. "I was raised in the mid-west. My parents owned a small lodge." She smiled in remembrance. "I used to love that place. It was like always being on holiday." A frown replaced the smile. "Then, one day, my mother just up and left us. I was nine. I never saw her again. Things got rough after that. I helped out at the lodge because my father needed me. I'd watched my mother so many times, it came easy." Pain filled her eyes. "I used to make up stories about her. I told people she was dead so they wouldn't know she'd loved us so little she'd run away from us. A year and a half after she left, my father remarried. We'd managed to hold onto the lodge he and I. When he got married again, I still helped out with the lodge, but now it was because I was being made to by a woman who was taking my mother's place. I never accepted that, or her."

She turned to face him. "My stepmother was a hard woman. She liked things done just so, and her way. The marriage lasted five years. She and my father had a son. I resented him. My father and my stepmother fought a lot. His fault, I think. Like me, he never really got over my mother. He died when I was seventeen, a few months after Ev and I were married."

Frank wasn't sure what he'd expected, but he knew he hadn't expected a background such as she's outlined. He'd figured she'd been raised more gently, unexposed to hardship.

"You said you had a brother. Could Derek be with him?"

"No, Derek never knew my half brother, or like me, where to find him. We lost touch when my father and stepmother separated."

"How did you meet your husband?"

She grinned. "At a ball game. I hated baseball. My girlfriend and I only went to them to meet boys."

He smiled. He loved her honesty. "You said you had some good years with Everett Hale."

She smiled. "You want to know if I loved him. I did. Very much, especially in those first few years. Oh, he was weak and too ambitious, even then, but I loved him enough to overlook those frailties. I'm not sure when I really stopped being in love with him and replaced that with just caring. Then, finally, acceptance of what he was. How about you?"

"You know just about everything about me there is to know."

"You mean all you wanted to tell me? Did you call Claire and tell her you were coming?"

"No."

"You can't keep running, Frank. Trust me, I know."

"I'll call her," he said impatiently.

"I hope so. Otherwise, why did you really come? I don't think it had so much to do with your old partner as it does with her."

It was the same question he'd been asking himself since they'd boarded the plane in Los Angeles.

***

They checked into a hotel. Frank played by Marian's rules. They took separate rooms.

Frank took a cab to the hospital where Andy had been admitted, promising Marian not to be gone too long. Traffic was bumper-to-bumper. He'd forgotten just how crowded New York streets were. The sounds of horns honking and angry drivers yelling at each other was strangely soothing. Once again he realized how much he'd missed this crazy, wonderful city.

Andy was in a room with three other men. He smiled when Frank entered the room. Frank drew the curtain around Andy's bed and took a seat beside it. When Andy extended his hand, Frank held it. "You're not looking bad, considering," Frank said. "Jenkins had me thinking you'd be in a straight jacket. Seriously, though, how goes it?"

Andy turned away. He was thinner than Frank remembered, old at forty. His cheeks were hollow, his lips thin. "Fuck Cordova, Frank. Four years ago he put me in a hospital, and now the son of a bitch has done it again."

Frank stood. "So beat him at his own game, Andy. For once, don't let him win. I speak from experience. The bastard has been in my head since...since Claire...since..."

"You can say her name, Frank. I miss Helen, but I never pretended that she wasn't dead."

Frank took Andy's hand again. He had a heartwarming feeling he was going to be all right. In some ways, Frank thought, he's stronger than I am because he gives into his weaknesses instead of fighting them. "Cordova got off easy, Andy. Neither of us will ever accept that, maybe, in time we'll learn to live with it."

"Thanks, Frank. I needed to hear that, and I needed to hear it from you. Do you stay in touch with Claire?"

"No."

"Too bad. Maybe you should find someone."

Frank wondered who was supposed to be comforting whom. He smiled. "I think I have. I brought her to New York with me."

Andy smiled back at him. It transformed his face. He no longer looked gaunt or even old. "Then what the hell are you doing here? Knowing you've made a new life for yourself is the best medicine I've had in years."

Frank squeezed Andy's hand. "That's good, but I can't live for both of us. You're going to have to make your own new life. Starting with getting out of here."

"I'll work on it."

"Promise?"

"Yeah, I promise."

"Great. I'll come back to see you before I leave town."

"No, you won't, because I don't want you to. Now, go on, get out of here. Go see your girl."

Frank looked back as he left the room. There was a satisfied smile on Andy's lips.

Frank was glad that he'd come.

***

Frank could hardly wait to show Marian his New York. Not just the Empire State building, the Statue of Liberty, and Ellis island and Broadway, but the life and heart of the city, the back streets, the garment district and the real people who made New York what it was. Yesterday, they'd driven across the Brooklyn Bridge, and they'd visited Coney Island, one of Frank's favorite spots.

What he hadn't done yet was make any attempt to see Claire.

Marian forced the issue. "You're running out of time, Frank. You have to see Claire and get it over with."

"Okay, okay, I'll do it."

"When?"

"Now. Is that what you want to hear?"

From the look on her face, Frank wasn't sure if Marian was pleased or upset. Jesus, when God made women he sure made them complicated!

He decided not to call Claire, but just show up on her doorstep. She and her husband had a small home outside Manhattan. He felt his heart begin to lurch when he drove up in front of the neatly maintained brick home. It was storybook perfect. A white picket fence surrounded the property. Kid's toys lay on the rich green lawn. Flowers bordered the freshly mowed grass.

It was everything he and Claire had talked about, but never gotten around to having. It had been a mistake to come here.

She answered the door herself. Her dark hair was pulled back with a green chiffon scarf that matched her eyes. She wore no make-up, her skin glowed. Her eyes widened in surprise. "Frank! What are you doing here? I thought you were in California."

He was sharply aware of her reticence. It was painful to know she was perceiving him as a possible threat. "Don't panic, Claire. I'm only here on a visit. Does it bother you so much that I wanted to see you while I was here?"

Her hesitation was momentary, but Frank saw it, and it hurt. "No. Of course not. I was getting ready to take Jordan to the park. Would you like to walk with us?"

Frank nodded. Jordan must be her son. "I'd like that."

She returned to the door a moment later, a blond haired child about six months old in her arms. Anxiety filled her eyes. She's remembering that I couldn't give her a child, Frank thought. She's afraid that his presence will make me feel inadequate. It does, he admitted. He smiled and reached out for the boy. He took his chubby fingers in his hand. "He looks like you, Claire."

"Not really." She pointed to a stroller in the halfway, "Would you mind?"

Frank wheeled the stroller down the front steps. Claire placed the child inside and strapped him in. "The park is only a few blocks away," she volunteered.

"Are you happy?" Frank blurted out. He cursed inwardly. He'd promised himself not to ask her that. Of course she's happy. She has everything she ever wanted. Everything I wasn't able to give her.

"Happiness is a relative thing, Frank. Jim is a good man, and he's a wonderful father."

"And when he comes home at night he doesn't bring his job with him."

"Wrong." She smiled. "He often brings his accounts home."

"There's a difference."

She sighed. "Yes, there's a difference."

They had reached the park. Claire stopped at a bench. "Let's sit for a while?"

Frank took a seat beside her making sure to leave room between them.

"Why did you come back to New York, Frank?"

"To see Andy and to exorcize some ghosts."

"Cordova?"

"For one. I realize now that I really came to see how I felt about you."

She turned away from him. "I don't think I want to know the answer to that."

"You already do. You must have read my feelings in my face back at the house. When you answered the door it was as if time had stood still. I felt the same way I did all those years ago when I first met you. Breathless."

"Don't, Frank, please."

"I know. I'm your past, and you have to be mine. I accept that. It doesn't mean I like it, but I accept it. I've met someone. Her name is Marian."

"Is it serious?"

"There are moments when I think it is."

Moisture filled her eyes. "I want you to be happy, Frank. You deserve to be. You're a good man. Don't tell her how you think you feel about me."

"Why not?"

"Two reasons. One, I'm not sure you're not just hanging onto something that is no more real than your desire for it to be. Even if that isn't true, for once in your life be human enough to tell a protective lie when it's best for everyone."

Frank didn't want to think about what he was going to tell Marian about his visit with Claire. Not now. Not at this moment. Not here with Claire by his side. "I'd like you to meet Marian."

Claire hesitated. "Are you looking for my approval?"

He flushed. He had been guilty of wanting that?. "No, just to meet her."

She searched his face, looking for reassurance. "How much longer will you be in New York?"

"Two more days."

Resolution took hold. "Then come to dinner tomorrow evening. You can meet Jim."

And see how happy you are, Frank thought. He felt an invisible knife embedded in his back. "Okay."

"Good. About seven?"

"Sure."

They stood and stared at each other, the electricity between them more intimate than any touch.

"I wish it could have been different for us," he said.

"So do I. But life goes on."

The baby started to whimper. "Walk me back to the house."

Halfway there, he said, "Do you still have dreams about Cordova?"

A shadow passed over her face. "Yes. I guess I always will. It helps to know he can't ever hurt anyone ever again."

"I wish I could be so sure," Frank said.

Claire stopped in her tracks. "Cordova is dead, Frank!"

"Is he? Then why do I still feel like he's still alive?"

Concern etched lined in her face. "Because you won't let go, Frank, and you have to."

He smashed a fist into the palm of his other hand. "Suicide. That's too fucking easy. I wanted the son of a bitch to pay a higher price for what he did to you."

"For a long time, so did I. I've come to terms with what happened. Now, you have to."

Easy to say. Suddenly, his being here seemed all wrong. "Listen, maybe dinner tomorrow night isn't such a great idea."

She sighed. "I think it is. Possibly necessary. You aren't the only one who needs to put the past to bed."

***

It was painfully obvious to Frank that Claire and Marian didn't like each other. Even more surprising was the fact that he and Jim did. Frank had expected to resent the man who had taken his place with Claire. Instead, he found that he was a little sorry for him, because while Claire might be happy with her life, it was obvious she wasn't in love with the man she'd married. In some respects, Frank grudgingly admitted, it was possible that the fact that she really liked him, and trusted him, was much better. At least as far as Claire was concerned.

The bottom line, Frank conceded, was that when Jim Hartford woke up in the morning it was with the knowledge that Claire would be lying beside him, and when he came home at night she would be waiting for him.

Frank and Jim tried to pretend the hostility, however vague and well concealed, was not hovering like a dark cloud over the two women's heads. Frank looked from one to the other. One of whom he loved, the other he cared for, just how much he didn't know yet. One was his past. The other, his future if he'd let her be. He realized now that he'd been mistaken when he'd thought Marian was another Claire. Seeing them side by side, comparing their movements, their reactions, he knew they were not alike at all. He wondered now what had made him think they were.

It was a relief for everyone when the evening was over. Back at their hotel Marian made an effort to make up for what at best could be called a tense evening.

"I like Claire," she said.

"Bullshit."

Marian flushed. "All right. So I don't like her. In case you didn't notice, the feeling is mutual."

"I noticed."

"You're still in love with her," Marian accused.

He didn't bother denying her accusation. "It was your idea for me to see her, not mine."

"Then it's true!"

"Even if it is, it doesn't matter. Claire is my past. I can deal with that now."

"I wonder if she can."

"What in the hell is that supposed to mean?"

"That she's still in love with you, too."

"That's crazy."

"Is it?"

Frank jerked off his tie and threw it on the chair by the bed. "What do you want me to do about it?"

"Anything you can. I didn't think I'd ever say this, but I'll take the pieces of you that you can spare for as long as I can deal with it, but I have to believe that when you're making love to me, you're not thinking about Claire. Is that so much to ask?"

He knew it wasn't. All he had to do was walk away from a past that had never done anything but hurt him.

He crooked his finger. "Come here."

She moved closer. Frank took her in his arms. "Give me time, Marian, and try to give me some space. I think I might be in love with you."

She clung to him. "God help me," she whispered. "I KNOW I'm in love with you.

***

Claire called Frank at the hotel early the next morning. She wanted to see him before he and Marian left New York the next day. She suggested the park. He lied to Marian and told her the call was from one of his former colleagues.

If Marian suspected he was lying, she didn't say so. She volunteered to spend the morning doing some last minute sightseeing alone.

Claire was waiting for him at the park, sitting on the same bench. She was nudging the stroller back and forth. Jordan was asleep.

Frank sat down beside her. "I shouldn't be here."

She nodded. "I know, but I had to talk to you. We walk different paths now, you and I, but that doesn't mean I've stopped caring." When he started to speak, she checked him. "Don't misunderstand me. I wouldn't trade my life. I can cope with what I have. It's you I'm worried about."

"Why?"

She took his hand. "I want you to have what's best for you, Frank. I know I said you should make a life with Marian, but that was before I met her. I don't like her."

He pulled his hand away. "That was obvious. So, you don't like Marian. It was stupid of me to think it was important that you should. Then again, maybe you're just jealous"

She blushed. "You're right. I sound like a jealous wife. I just don't want you to get hurt again."

He stared at her, longing in his eyes. All she had to do was tell him she'd come back to him. She had to know that. Just as surely as he knew she wasn't going to say the words he longed to hear. "I thought I'd go see the guys at the precinct."

"Another loose end?"

It was the second lie he'd told today. He had no intention of going by the precinct. "Yeah, another loose end." He reached over and took her face in his hands. He gently kissed her. "Stay happy, Claire." He patted the sleeping child's golden curls, regret in his eyes. "He's a great kid."

She was still sitting there when he left her. He didn't look backward. He knew he could never look backward as far as Claire was concerned. In a day or so he would be leaving the East coast, leaving Claire behind, for good this time.

***

"Just one more day," Frank said. "We'll drive to Tenafly, New Jersey, and take a flight to California from there."

"It's not the change in flights that bothers me, it's this thing with Cordova," Marian answered. "You said he was dead. What possible purpose would your going to the mental institution serve? You didn't get enough of places like that when you went to see your friend, Andy?"

"I don't know what purpose it will serve. Maybe none. I only know I have to go. For me, and for Andy." He smiled. "Hey, weren't you the one who said I had to bury my ghosts? In some respects Cordova has a bigger hold on my past than Claire."

She frowned. "What if you can't shake that hold?"

"Then, like my feelings for Claire, I'll deal with the situation. Okay?"

She didn't look convinced. One thing this trip to New York had taught her was that once Frank set his mind to something, nothing and no one was going to change it.

They checked into a motel outside of Tenafly, about five miles from the institution where Cordova had spent his last days. Again, they had separate rooms.

"Come with me," Frank urged, as he prepared to leave for the mental institution.

Marian turned away from him. "I can't. I don't agree with what you're doing. I certainly don't understand your reasons. No, if you insist on going to that place, you're going to have to do it alone."

The building was a sterile white two-story structure. It was situated on three acres of manicured grounds. Disorientated men talked to imaginary companions as they walked the grounds under the watchful eyes of white-suited attendants. The institution house only the adjudged criminally insane, or those deemed to have the tendencies.

Frank shuddered. Cordova must have hated it here. These men were obviously beyond help, while Cordova was for all intents and purposes, at least on the surface, as sane as most of the people free to walk the streets.

He was escorted to the administration building by an attendant, then led down to the hall to a door marked JOHN REEVER, CHIEF ADMINISTRATOR. The attendant knocked on the door, and was allowed admission. He ushered Frank inside.

John Reever was a small man in his early fifties. He motioned Frank to a chair by his desk.

"What brings you here, Detective Damien?"

"Michael Cordova."

"Cordova is dead."

"Yes, I know."

"You wish to know how he died?"

Frank shook his head. "I already know how." He nodded toward the window. The courtyard was visible, as were the lost souls who paraded around it. "I think I know why. This place must have seemed like a living death to a man like Cordova."

"Then what exactly is it you think I can do for you?"

"I want to see the room Cordova occupied."

Reever folded his hands together. "Cordova mentioned you...often. Sometimes his anger against you was uncontrollable. Other times, he seemed almost fond of you. Yet, when our people tried to get at the root of his relationship with you, he removed himself to an unreachable level. I suppose you understand the reasons why."

Frank violently shook his head. "No, I don't. Can I see his room?"

Reever stood and moved to a filing cabinet. "I see that we've placed no one else in that room as yet. Tell me, what do you hope to achieve by visiting his room?"

"I haven't a clue."

Reever slammed the cabinet shut. "There are all kinds of madness, Detective Damien. Maybe you should examine your motives."

Frank felt a chill pass over him. "I'm not crazy, Mr. Reever. Or is it Doctor Reever?"

He smiled. "It's Doctor Reever."

"Like I said I'm not crazy."

Reever sighed. "Don't worry. I don't believe you are...yet," he added grimly. "All right, it's unorthodox, but I'll allow you a few minutes in Cordova's room. A few minutes only," he warned. He reached for the phone and gave orders for one of the attendants to return. "I'll have someone take you there."

Cordova's room was in a small wing at the end of the complex. The sound of the door closing on Cordova's room sounded like thunder to Frank's ears. There were no personal effects left. They'd been removed right after Cordova died. The walls were pastel blue, a color some psychiatric experts maintained had a calming effect on violent patients. Only Cordova hadn't been violent in the usual sense of the work, just his acts.

The room held a hospital bed, a bedside table with a Bible atop it, a chest of drawers, a round table with four chairs, and a portable television.

Something else Frank found both frightening and disarming. Cordova might be dead, but his presence still filled the room.

Frank shook himself. This was a room like all the others in this institution. And you don't believe in spirits, he reminded himself. He suddenly needed air. He moved to the door, and reached for the handle. It wouldn't open. Sweat began to bead on his forehead. I have to get out of here, he thought wildly. He banged on the door. It opened. Reever stood on the other side. He noted the rivulets of moisture on Frank's brow.

"Are you all right?" he asked.

Frank struggled to maintain his composure. "Yeah, I'm fine. For a moment I thought the door was locked."

"It sticks sometimes. I should have warned you. Did you find whatever you hoped for in here?"

"No."

"You did feel something. What was it?"

Frank shrugged impatiently. "Quit trying to psychoanalyze me, Doctor Reever. Cordova brutalized my wife before they caught him. I couldn't help thinking about it. That's all," he emphasized.

Marian was waiting for him back at the motel. "Well?" she asked.

"I'd rather not discuss it."

"Don't shut me out, Frank."

He shook his head. How could he possibly explain what he was feeling? How Cordova's room had turned him inside out. Or that despite the fact it was verifiable that Cordova was indeed dead, something about him still lived?

Frank and Marian flew back to California the following day. Despite Claire's reservations about Marion, that were maybe self-serving, Frank needed Marion, he told himself. Maybe with her help he could finally best the demons that lurked like shadowy threats around every corner.

CHAPTER 10

F rank's life was on hold. He knew that as long as the Hale case was open and unsolved it would go on that way.

There were others who wanted the Hale case closed. Most of them wanted to pin it on Cassady. Marian was among that number.

"Did you ever stop to think how simple and how wonderful-life could be if Ev's murder went away?" she'd asked. "Cassady's a confessed killer. Why isn't it possible that he could have killed Ev and Cleo?"

Frank shook his head. "It doesn't feel right."

"It doesn't feel right! That's a great statement. I assume you have more than that to go on?"

Frank shook his head. "You're just going to have to trust me."

She'd given him a look of disbelief, but in the end she'd reluctantly given way because he gave her no choice if she wanted to hang on to him.

His altercation with Marian led Frank once again to the principle players in the Hale murder case.

Miramba was first on his list. He went to see her on the set of her second Marvin Peters movie. The first picture was a resounding success, due largely to the fact that Miramba had several provocative nude scenes. Scenes that had had the censors and producer at each others throats. The ensuing publicity about the battle between the two powers had made her even more of a phenomenon.

She was clad in a bra and bikini briefs, overhead lights bearing down upon her. Her skin was like burnished gold. Despite himself, Frank began indulging himself in almost every man's fantasy. He wondered how it would feel to make love to her, and knew it would be an exciting, possibly an unforgettable experience. He hated himself for the momentary lapse. Whatever else their problems, he and Marian shared a healthy, satisfying, and frequent sex life even if it was still conducted at arms length. She still wouldn't spend the night with him. It was a condition of their relationship she refused to budge on, and, he allowed, a club to push the relationship into marriage.

Miramba left the spotlight and came toward him, a short robe carelessly tied around her, exposing the scanty bra and her spilling breasts. Recognition of his secret thought gleamed in her coal black eyes. She gave him a triumphant smile. "Detective Damien! I would say this is a pleasant surprise, but I think I expected you to show up sooner or later. You're like a bad penny." She tossed back her long frizzy curls and winked at him. "I'm finished for the day. Follow me to my trailer and we can talk." She arched her brows. "You are here to talk to me, aren't you?"

She was confident of her appeal and it galled him. "Tell me, Miramba. Does every man you meet fall all over himself trying to get you between the sheets?"

She smiled. "Almost without exception. I think possibly you are that exception. I heard that you and Marian Hale are seeing each other."

"If I was it wouldn't be any of your business."

She seemed pleased at his reaction. "My, aren't we touchy?"

The vehicle that served as Miramba's mobile dressing room was more than just a home on wheels. It was a shrine to her. The furnishings, as elaborate as they were, took a back seat to the pictures on the walls. There wasn't one square inch of space that didn't contain a life size picture of Miramba. The one that drew his immediate attention was the one that was most prominently displayed. She was completely nude, her fingers trailing her sex. Nothing was left to the imagination.

She followed his gaze. "Do you like it?"

"From one of Peter's movies?"

She laughed. "No. Playboy. The complete layout will appear in next month's issue."

Frank shook his head. "You're a talented actress, so the critics say, anyway. And you're a gifted singer. Why do a spread for Playboy? You don't need it."

She laughed again. "You think it will ruin my career? Unlike the Monroe's, the Vanessa's, the Suzanne Sommers of this world, my successful career was launched, a la Joan Collins. Except I went a step further than Joan."

"Only one step?"

She stretched. Her breasts threatened to escape their flimsy casing.

"I'm bored of this conversation. You didn't come here to discuss my morals." She laughed. "If you had, it would be a damned short conversation. Why did you come, Damien? No, let me guess. You came here because your girlfriend is upset with me."

Frank wondered how in the hell Miramba had known about him and Marian. "What in the hell would Marian have to be angry with you about?"

Miramba reached for a cigarette. She offered the pack to Frank. He took one, lit hers, then his own. She blew smoke into the air. "I see that Joanna hasn't told you, or her mother."

Joanna wouldn't have told him anything. "Told us what?"

"Oh dear, I see I've let the cat out of the bag. There's a small part in my picture that Joanna would be perfect for."

"Joanna?"

"Yes," Miramba impatiently answered. "Joanna."

"I didn't know you knew her that well."

"I don't, but the kid has a schoolgirl-like celebrity complex. Everett's fault. He tried to keep his children away from the business. All that did was make his daughter want it all the more." There was a soft wistful tone in her voice as she added, "She's a beautiful child." She smiled. "The world likes beauty. Especially in this town. She wrote me a letter recently, care of Doug. He passed it on to me. I suppose her letter amused him. She asked for my help to get her a career as an actress started. I confess her letter amused me, too. Everett made a good living from celebrities, yet the pious son of a bitch thought his kids were too good for the business. He certainly never wanted them around the likes of me."

It occurred to Frank that Miramba had a penchant for more than young men. He felt his blood begin to boil. How was Marian going to react to this unexpected piece of news? He was losing perpective. Forgetting my real reason for being here, he reminded himself. "I'll talk to Marian. I'm sure she won't allow Joanna to take part in any movie. Let alone one of yours. However," he added, "Joanna isn't the reason I came to see you. I cam e about a kid named Darryl Cassady."

She frowned. "Cassady? The man who confessed to killing those people in San Diego? The same man who may have killed my sister?"

"That's a debatable point. I searched Cassady's apartment before we brought him in. He had several pictures signed, "To Darryl with love, Miramba."

"Is that what brought you here?" she said incredulously. "A few pictures? Do you have any idea how many of those damn things I sign? Half the country has at least one that says to somebody, love Miramba."

"I had the feeling it was more than that. We never did find the young stud you claimed to have been with the night your sister was killed."

She looked shocked, giving what Frank considered a command performance. Then she was an actress, he considered, a credible one by most accounts. "Confess, Detective Damien. You want those pictures to mean more. You're still after Doug's ass. What are you trying to say? That Doug and I hired this maniac to kill my sister and her husband?"

"Your suggestion, Miramba, not mine. It's an interesting scenario, don't you think?

"Go straight to hell, Damien. Doug was released for lack of evidence, and you have nothing on me. I didn't kill Cleo. For God's sake, she was my sister. My flesh and blood."

"And she was after something you wanted."

"Marvin's picture! She didn't stand a chance."

"Maybe Cleo didn't see it that way."

"Like I said, go straight to hell."

Frank smiled. He turned to leave. He'd riled her. On its own it meant nothing, but it gave him a sense of satisfaction he hadn't felt in a long time.

She had the last word, however.

"Tell that girlfriend of yours," Miramba yelled after him, "that her daughter is over eighteen. If Joanna wants a career in show business she's not going to give up on it. If I can help her, I'll be happy to do it. Tell THAT to Marian Hale."

Marian was furious. "This is incredible. I knew Joanna was star struck, but this is ridiculous." She gave Frank an accusing glance. "I don't suppose it has occurred to you that Miramba is helping Joanna toward that goal as a way of getting back at you for dogging her about Ev and Cleo?"

"Me! It seems to me that Joanna instigated this entire episode all by herself."

"You couldn't and still can't leave Beck and Miramba alone, can you? Have you completely forgotten about Cassady in your obsession to get Doug Beck?"

They were still staring angrily at each other when Joanna came bursting through the front door. She observed the glares re-directed her way. "Trouble in paradise?" She asked.

"Come here, young lady," Marian commanded.

Joanna entered the living room, threw her purse and a package on the couch, and said. "What did I do now?"

Marian prodded her daughter into the closet chair. "How long have you been communicating with Miramba?"

She sighed. "So, that's it. I was going to tell you." She gave Frank a hard look. "But then you've been kind of busy lately."

"Stop it!" Marian said. "Don't use Frank or myself to justify what you've done."

Frank smiled inwardly. A moment ago Marian was ready to attack him for his part in Joanna's actions. Now she was defending him. Women! Go figure!

"I forbid you going to Hollywood," Marian continued.

Joanna stood. "I knew you would, that's why I didn't tell you about the movie. I'm eighteen, Mother. That means that legally I can do what the hell I want." She threw up her hands. "I suppose this means you'll want me out of here. I'll go pack. I can probably stay with Miramba temporarily."

It looked like Marian was set to strike her. Frank stepped in between the two of them. "When I first met you, Joanna, you were just an avid fan. Now, it seems you and Miramba are soul mates. How did that happen?"

"I don't have to answer to you."

"I think you do," Marian said quietly, her anger now controlled but not dissipated. "As a matter of fact I'd like to know the answer to that myself."

Joanna shrugged. "It's no big deal. I began to contact Miramba right after Daddy was killed. You didn't seem to give a damn that he was dead. Then nothing cracks that cool façade, does it Mother? Miramba was nice enough to write back to me. She even remembered me, which was a surprise. We'd only met once. Then only briefly."

"And, Beck?" Frank questioned. "Had you met him, too?"

"Frank!" Marian intervened.

"It's okay, Mother. It's the cop in him. He can't help himself. I told you that first day that I hadn't met Doug Beck. I wrote to Miramba in care of him because it's common knowledge he's her agent. I guess I'll meet him now. Miramba thinks he'll take me on as a client."

"For God's sake, Joanna," Frank exploded. "Beck may have killed your father. It's even possible that Miramba helped him to do it."

Joanna turned on her mother. "He's crazy. They have Daddy's killer in custody, don't they?" There was a wave of uncertainty in her voice.

Marian avoided looking at Frank. "Yes, I think it's possible they do."

Relief filled Joanna's voice. "Then, that's that. I'll go pack."

After Joanna left the room, Frank said. "That was real cute. You might have stopped her if she thought Beck had something to do with her father's death."

When she didn't respond, Frank added. "Go up and see her, Marian. I don't think you have a prayer of changing her mind about pursuing a show business career, but you can tell her this is still her home. If she leaves here like this, if she leaves here angry, she may never come back. Her association with Miramba is more than just undesirable, it's unhealthy."

"What do you mean?"

Frank thought about the look in Miramba's eyes when she'd spoken Joanna's name. "Miramba likes young sex. I don't think she limits herself to young men."

Marian paled. She started to say something, then moved toward the hallway and practically ran up the stairs.

***

It had been a peaceful day at the Santa Barbara police station with only a few misdemeanors. Frank and Marian had a quiet dinner on the pier. Joanna had left yesterday with promises to call home when she got settled. She'd made further promises to come back home as soon as her small role in Miramba's movie was complete. Frank suspected that neither Marian or Joanna really believed that.

After dinner they strolled along the beach. Although it was unspoken, they both knew they wouldn't have sex tonight. Tonight, sex would be replaced by something more valuable, companionship.

Frank took her hand in his. "She'll be okay, Marian. You gave her a set of values that will stay with her."

She stopped and kissed his cheek. "Thank you for that, but I really messed things up, didn't I? I couldn't sustain a marriage with my children's father, I built a wall up so high Joanna couldn't scale it, and I failed my son so that he felt it necessary to run away."

"You're being too hard on yourself. Everett Hale was a tough case by all accounts. It takes two to make a marriage work. As for Joanna, you weren't the only influence in her life. You didn't fail her. She just feels the need to try her wings. Derek is something else. I gotta admit I don't know how to make you feel any better about him. I wish the little bastard would turn himself in."

"He's not a criminal, Frank, he's just scared. He has to be, else he'd come home. We were very close," she offered. "He needed me more than either Ev or Joanna ever could." A smile crossed her face. "My poor ugly duckling. He wouldn't believe that someday, like a moth, he would turn into a butterfly." There was a catch in her voice as she added, "Where is he, Frank?"

"I don't know. Since Cleo's ring surfaced there's been all out effort to bring him to ground. At least there was," he said bitterly. "Time's our enemy. The longer it goes before we find him, and the longer it goes before we can nail Beck, the chances of us ever doing either is slim. Every day that passes, makes solving your ex-husband's murder that much less of a priority." He grimaced. "I may be the only one left who really cares about the truth."

She folded herself into his warmth. "Why can't it just be over? Why can't we just have ourselves to worry about? Why can't we..." Her voice trailed off in a sigh.

He knew she was gong to say why can't we be married? He wasn't ready. He knew he wouldn't be ready until he found the person or persons, responsible for the death of Everett and Cleo Hale. It was an obsession that overshadowed and outweighed his feelings for her.

***

Sheila Beck made an attempt to slam the door on Frank. His foot in the doorway prevented her from it.

"Please, Mrs. Beck," he gently responded. "I didn't come here to hurt you."

"You want to hurt Doug," she accused.

"I only want the truth. Nothing more. Please, let me come in for a moment. I won't stay long. I promise."

She reluctantly opened the door wider. "Just a few moments. Then you have to leave."

She didn't invite Frank to be seated. "Doug would be angry if he knew I was talking to you."

"Why? Because he's afraid you might let something slip?"

A determined look passed over her face. "There's nothing to let slip. I wish you'd leave us alone. Doug didn't kill those people."

It's hopeless, Frank thought. The woman has no backbone. "Okay. I'll go." He stopped at the door. "How's the marriage working out?"

She bit her lip. "It's fine."

Any fool could see she was lying. "I'm sorry."

She determinedly stuck out her chin. "It isn't over yet."

"Yeah, well good luck."

She was going to need it, Frank decided.

Frank stopped by the studio lot. Peters waved at him. Miramba was on stage with a muscled young man. She was arguing with him, her hands on her lap, her nostrils flared, hey eyes black pools of hatred. The man raised his hand to slap her. She grabbed his wrist. He twisted hers in response and forced her to her knees. He knelt beside her. She spat in his face.

Peters yelled, "Cut." He rubbed his hands together. "That was wonderful, Darling, and only one take! Let's take a break."

Miramba exited the spotlight.

Off in the shadows Frank saw the reason he was here today. Joanna was sitting offstage her knees drawn up to her chest. She looked so much younger than her eighteen years and heart wrenchingly vulnerable.

She looked up as Frank approached her, surprise on her face, which quickly turned to contempt. "Spying on me?"

"No. Just seeing if you're all right."

"Don't tell me you care?"

"Is that so surprising?"

She ignored his attempt to get close to her. "Did you see that last scene?" Her eyes lit up with excitement. "She's marvelous, isn't she?"

Frank was hard pressed to argue. Miramba had been damned convincing. So much so he hadn't been sure until Peers had yelled cut that she was only acting. "Okay, so she's good. How about you? Have you shot any of your scenes yet?"

"You mean scene! No, not yet. I only have two lines, but it's a start," she added defiantly. "More than most people without experience ever get."

"I don't know how to ask you this. I guess there's no easy way. I'm concerned about that one scene. Is there anything in it that will make your mother ashamed?"

"You mean do I take my clothes off? No. I don't.

Frank sighed. "I'm glad. Thanks for telling me the truth. You could have played hardball."

He was on his way out when he felt a hand on his shoulder. It was Joanna. "How is my mother? How's she taking my leaving?"

"So-so. She's feeling guilty. She's blaming herself for the wall she erected between the two of you. She's condemning herself for favoring Derek because she felt sorry for his lack of personal appeal." He shrugged. "Other than that she's just fine." He smiled. "Come home once in a while, Joanna. Give her a chance to make up for what she sees as her failings."

Joanna tilted her head to one side. "You really care about her, don't you?"

"Of course I do. What did you think?"

"I guess I didn't think. I was too busy resenting you."

He smiled and brushed his lips across her cheek. "I know. That makes two of us."

She looked over her shoulder. There was activity on stage. "I'd better go back in. Miramba arranged for me to present on the set whenever I wanted to be. It's an opportunity of a lifetime." She started to move away, then said, "Go see my Uncle Jed. I think he knows more about Derek's disappearance than he told the police."

Frank stared thoughtfully after her. He wondered how much more she knew and hadn't told.

***

Frank hadn't seen Jed Hale since Beck's trial. The apartment building looked, if possible, even more desolate.

Hale opened the door, hesitated, stepped back, and invited Frank inside. The familiar smell of stale tobacco and liquor assailed his nostrils.

"What makes me think this isn't just a friendly visit, Damien?"

"Maybe it's your protective instinct. I just came from seeing Joanna. She thinks you know something about her brother's disappearance."

Hale moved to the kitchen. He opened a cabinet, took out a half empty bottle of cheap Scotch and poured himself a glassful. He took a swallow, raised the bottle and offered it to Frank. Frank shook his head.

Hale returned to the small cluttered living room. He took another swig of scotch. He shuddered. "I remember when I only drank the best. Ah, yes, Joanna. She always was more like her father, now, she seems bent on proving it. Hollywood," he snorted. "The devil's playground."

"About Derek?" Frank prompted.

"What about him?"

"Do you know where he is?"

Hale lifted his glass and drained it. "I told the other cops everything I knew when they came here, which is nothing."

Frank played a hunch. "You were close to the boy, weren't you?"

"Someone had to be. Marian tried, but he needed a man. He needed a father. Everett was never there for him, so I filled the void when I could."

"Did he come to see you before he took off?"

Hale gave Frank a hard look. He seemed to be weighing his next words. When he answered, Frank was sure he wasn't telling the truth.

"He was here the day before he left. He came here a lot. That particular day we talked just like always. Nothing special. Nothing to indicate he was leaving home?"

Frank sighed. "I think his visit to you entailed more than that. If that's true, you're a real bastard. Marian has gone through hell wondering where he is, not knowing if he's alive or dead."

"What do you care?"

"I care. Let's just leave it at that."

Animosity filled Hale's voice. "So you say. Not enough to marry her, right?"

Frank stared at him. Jesus! Hale was in love with Marian. He wondered if she knew, and how long Hale had coveted his brother's wife.

"How Marian and I handle our relationship and what we do with it is none of your goddamned business. I'll ask you once again, Hale. Do you know where the boy went?"

"No."

"No ideas?"

"None."

"I think you're lying."

Hale shrugged. "Think what you want."

Frank changed tactics. "I care for Marian. Very much. It bothers me when she's unhappy. Derek's absence makes her very unhappy."

Hale went back into the kitchen and poured himself another drink. "Come on, Detective, all you want to do is question the boy about Cleo's ring."

"I admit I want to talk to him about it, but I'm willing to give him the benefit of the doubt and assume he came by it innocently. Which is more than you seem to be willing to do, incidentally."

Hale emptied his glass. "You should have been a social worker. You're a regular bleeding heart. If you really cared about Marian you'd stay the hell out of Everett's murder. She'd like to put Everett's death behind her, but you won't let her. Maybe you should spend more time with her and less time hassling people. Try acting like a man who cares about Marian instead of just bragging about it."

There were several ways Hale could have known about Frank's obsession with the Hale case. The most likely way, of course, was from

Marian, which meant she and Hale had discussed the problem. Frank didn't like Hale. He realized that he'd never liked him, but he had to admit that Hale had a point. With that observation came another realization. If Hale really did know something about Derek's disappearance, Frank was the last person he was going to tell.

CHAPTER 11

Frank paced the corridor of the UCLA Medical Center. He checked his watch: 11:29 p.m.

He thought about the call that had brought him here, wondering still why the girl who had almost lost her life, had called him of all people.

A white uniformed nurse, not much older than the girl inside the room she'd just come from, approached him, a professional smile on her plump but pretty face. "Mr. Damien?"

He nodded.

"She's asking for you. Don't stay long," she cautioned. "She needs rest."

She'd almost bought herself permanent rest, Frank thought ruefully as he entered the hospital room.

Frank took those first few precious seconds to study the girl who lay so deathly still in the bed. Her face was ashen, tears stained her cheeks. He couldn't stop the wave of sympathy that washed over him. Her gut must feel like hell after being subjected to the violent thrusts of a stomach pump.

She put out her hand. Frank hesitated, then took it.

"Thanks for coming," she said. "You must think it strange I'd ask for you, but I didn't know who else to call."

Frank patted her hand. "I'm glad you decided to call me. What about your mother? She should be here. She'd want to be here," he emphasized.

Joanna turned away. She buried her face in the pillow.

"I know. I will call her, I promise. I just needed to talk to someone who would understand what I did, and why. Someone who would be the least likely to condemn." She gave him a wan smile. "I immediately thought of you. In your line of work you must have dealt with numerous overdoses." She sighed. "I bet you've heard all the sob stories."

He squeezed her hand, hoping to give her reassurance. "Quite a few. What's yours?"

Joanna closed her eyes tightly, then slowly opened them. Pain was reflected there. "You knew about Miramba, didn't you?"

He'd hoped it wasn't going to get this ugly. "You want to talk about it?"

Joanna shook her head vigorously. "No. Not ever."

"Okay."

There was a heavy silence. "I have to. You know that too, of course."

Frank sighed. "Yeah, I do."

"There was this party," Joanna went on. "It was obvious there were drugs there. Miramba was high before my date and I arrived. We got separated. I never saw him again after that. Unless he was one of…" She swallowed hard. "Miramba tried to give me some pills. I refused them." Joanna shuddered. "I can still see the smile…it was evil, as she shoved a drink in my hand and said, "There, my little prude. A harmless glass of champagne." I took it," Joanna went on. "At first I thought it was the champagne that was making me feel strange. I'm not used to it. Oh, I'm no Puritan. I've drank before, but nothing stronger than beer or wine. The room began to spin." She laughed, the sound hollow. "I fell for the oldest trick in the book. The champagne must have been doctored."

She exerted so much pressure on Frank's hand his skin began to turn white.

"Go on," he encouraged.

"Miramba took me by the hand. We climbed some stairs. There seemed to be two of everything, that's why I'm not sure how many of them there were. It seemed like six or eight. I think, though, it must have been three or four. Two men, two women. And Miramba," she added, a catch in her voice. "They were all touching me. I was naked. Then it was just Miramba." Her next words tore raggedly from her throat. "Frank, why didn't you warn me?"

"I thought I tried. If I'd have been more specific, would you have believed me?"

"No," she replied, her voice barely above a whisper.

Frank removed his hand from hers. He stood. "What happened next?"

"Suddenly, I was alone. I threw up all over the bed. I groped for my clothes. There was a bottle of pills by the bed. I didn't care what they were. I just wanted to die. The next think I knew I was being wheeled down a hospital corridor. People were yelling. Someone asked who I wanted to call. I gave them your name."

Frank sighed. "I'm sorry you had to learn this kind of lesson the hard way. But then most kids do. You'll get over this episode, I promise you."

Tears filled her eyes and rolled down her cheeks. "I want to believe that."

"You can, and you can do me a favor."

"Anything."

"Lie to your mother, Joanna. Tell her your overdose was accidental. Leave out the part about Miramba and the orgy."

She winced at the word "orgy" and released his hand. Frank cursed himself for his thoughtlessness, for using words that were natural to a cop. Words that were unwarranted as a father figure, a role he'd reluctantly assumed when he'd entered this room.

"She doesn't need to know, Joanna. If you'd really thought she did, you wouldn't have called me."

Joanna nodded through her tears. "I won't tell her, I promise. Will you let her know I'm here?"

"Sure." His voice hardened. "Was Beck at the party?"

"No. He refused to handle me. Did you know that?"

Frank hadn't known. In fact, he would have bet money that Beck would have welcomed the chance to fuck up Joanna's life any way he could, to spite him.

She took his hand in hers again. "Thanks again for coming. It's funny, isn't it? I trust you, but I must be honest, I'm still not sure that I like you." She frowned. "What does that make me?"

He smiled. "It makes you human. Now get some rest."

As he left the hospital it occurred to Frank that maybe he wasn't such a bad father figure after all.

***

Joanna came home after a few days. Marian picked her up at the hospital. Frank suspected the mother-daughter relationship they were experiencing was the best they'd ever had. In a strange but satisfying way, he felt partially responsible for the serenity that now filled the house on Chapparal Street.

Joanna stayed for a month. Frank arrived at the house one evening and was met with the information that Joanna was leaving for New York the next day.

"New York?" he asked Marian. "What the hell is in New York?"

Joanna came into the room. "I want to study acting, Frank. I don't want any more handouts like the one Miramba gave me. I want to make it on my own. I want to start at the bottom like everyone else. No more shortcuts."

"Do you have to go four-thousand miles from here?"

"There's a good school in New York, and it's time I stood on my own two feet." She smiled. "Besides, you and Mother could stand some time alone."

Frank turned to Marian. "You want her to go to New York!"

"Yes, and no. I admit I wish Joanne would choose another career, but she's set on this one." She gave him a rueful smile. "I almost lost her once already because I tried to live her life for her. I won't do it again." She smiled over at Joanna. "At least I'll try not to. I've arranged for a loan against the trust fund Ev left the children. I've agreed to pay a years acting tuition. After that, we'll see."

Frank managed a few moments alone with Joanna before she left. She was in her room throwing some last minute items in her suitcase. She smiled over at him. "Thanks for not spilling the beans on me."

"You were worried about it? I thought you trusted me."

She laughed. "I did say that, didn't I? I think I might even like you a little."

"I'm glad. You're kinda growing on me, too. Seriously. There are drugs in New York, too, Joanna, and far worse things. You think what happened with Miramba was bad..."

Joanna slammed the lid of her suitcase. "Mom said you'd feel obligated to give me this lecture." She sat on the edge of her bed. "Go ahead."

"This is no laughing matter, Joanna, and your mother doesn't know what we know. Believe me, whatever you found in Hollywood you'll find in spades in New York."

"Mom also said your view of New York was jaded. Trust me, Frank," she said. "Trust me to take care of myself."

"Do I have a choice?"

She smiled. "No."

He stood on the threshold of the room. "I went to see your uncle. He denied knowing anything about Derek's disappearance."

"I guess I'm not too surprised. He and Derek were soul mates. I used to joke about it. I called them the intellectual and the bum." She sobered. "Somehow that doesn't seem so funny now." She shrugged. "My feeling that my Uncle Jed knew anything was just that, a feeling."

"Are you sure you're not holding something back from me?"

"Nothing."

Frank stared into her eyes. He saw only truth mirrored there.

***

Joanna had been gone for three weeks. Frank and Marian were curled up on the sofa in his apartment watching a sitcom on television. Frank liked them. They were usually so ridiculously far-fetched, so far removed from real life, they proved to be a great escape for him. Marian, on the other hand, only tolerated such shows for his sake. She preferred serious dramas.

Frank leaned over to kiss her during a news break. He froze in motion.

"This is Katie Couric with a news break. This evening, at a suburban residence where a Hollywood party was underway, Miramba, the well-known singer and actress, was wounded, when a woman named Sheila Beck crashed the party armed with a pistol. Also wounded, and in critical condition, is the assailant's husband, Doug Beck, Miramba's agent. Doug Beck, as you may recall, was arrested, then released in connection with the murders of Everett and Cleo Hale. Cleo Hale was Miramba's sister."

Frank stared at the television screen. Katie Couric smiled at the camera and said, "More news at eleven."

He jumped up from the couch. He took several long strides to the phone. He looked back at Marian. Concern etched worry lines in her face. She's begun to believe my obsession with her ex-husband's murder is over, he thought. It might have been, he allowed, except for the events of this evening. He held the receiver in his hand, indecision wracking his face. He muttered an apology as he looked away from her accusing glare and dialed Captain Markham's home number.

Cliff Markham answered. "Hello."

"Cliff. Did you see the news?"

The Captain's tone was guarded. "I didn't have to. I got a call about the shooting when it came over the teletype."

"You didn't call me!"

Markham sighed. "No, I didn't. I knew if I waited long enough you'd call me."

Frank cursed under his breath. The Hale murder case was all but dead. Markham and everyone else wanted it to go away. "What hospital did they take them to?"

"UCLA."

"Are they alive?"

"Last I heard. Miramba is out of danger. Beck is still critical, though. I don't think you should..." Markham stared at the phone, listening to the dial tone.

He turned to his wife, Christine. "Crazy son of a bitch. I like him, I just don't understand him. Sometimes I think he never got over that case in New York I told you about. The one where his wife was almost killed. The Hale killings have become his obsession, almost as if they'd taken the place of that other incident." He sighed. "Just lately, I'd thought he was over that obsession. Seems I was wrong."

***

Marian followed Frank to the door. He was shrugging on his jacket, grabbing his car keys.

"Do you really have to go?" she asked.

He nodded.

"I guess I knew the answer to that question before I asked it. "If you still believe that Cassidy didn't kill Everett and Cleo, and if you think Beck really killed them, I suppose I can understand your need to see him, or at least I can try to. If you're wrong, Frank, walk away from it. Promise me you'll do that."

He knew if he stayed at moment longer he might weaken and make a promise he had no guarantee he could keep. He leaned over and gave her a perfunctory kiss, his mind racing ahead. "You sure you don't want me to drop you off at the house?"

She shook her head. "No. I'll wait for you here."

His indecision increased. He gave her a longer more lingering kiss. "Thanks. I'd like that."

Marian watched him traverse the walkway that led to the garages. For weeks now she'd known true contentment. She loved Frank more than she'd ever dared hope to love anyone ever again. She'd begun to hope that this blissful interlude that had lasted for so long was marking a promising new beginning for them.

She was beginning to understand why Claire had found it necessary to leave him. She closed the door to the apartment and took her place on the couch, staring vacantly at the television screen. She'd faced the harsh reality a long time ago that it took fortitude and dedication to stay with a man like Frank.

Every day she fervently hoped she was up to the challenge.

CHAPTER 12

The hospital parking lot and foyer were crawling with media personnel. Frank walked past the horde of reporters. They gave him only a cursory glance. He thanked God that his involvement in the Hale murders hadn't warranted more than minimal media attention.

He flashed his badge at the blonde switchboard operator who doubled as a receptionist at this late hour. "Doug Beck, and Miramba?" he inquired. "Which floor are they on?"

She made no pretense of looking for the information he sought on the room chart to her left. The question had been asked so many times this evening she knew the answer by heart. "Mr. Beck is in intensive care. Miramba is on the fourth floor. Men from your department are already upstairs."

Frank didn't correct the assumption that he was part of the Southern California police detail assigned to the shootings. He moved toward the elevator.

His first stop was intensive care. The problem of how to get past the assigned police unit was solved when Frank saw Ben Allandro among their number. He walked over to him, acutely aware of the guarded looks thrown his way by the other three men.

"It's okay, Allandro said. "This is Frank Damien from Santa Barbara. I worked with him on the Hale case when Beck was a suspect."

A tall spare man, obviously Allandro's superior officer, said, "What brings you here, Damien?"

"I have my reasons. Can I talk to you privately?"

"Sure." He extended his hand. "Lieutenant Larry Cranville."

The lieutenant moved down the hall with Frank. He stopped at a vending machine and put two quarters in the slot. "Coffee?"

Frank shook his head.

Cranville placed the hot liquid to his lips. He grimaced. "Jesus! The coffee is as bad as the food." He grinned. "I spent a few days here last year. Burst appendicitis. What's on your mind, Damien?"

"Doug Beck. I never made any secret that I wasn't happy about his release in connection with the Hale killings. Beck was guilty in my book."

Cranville gave him a speculative look. "You weren't the only one with doubts at the time, as I recall. Then Cassady came along to fill the void left by Beck's release from custody. You don't buy the fact that Cassady killed the Hale couple as well as the Rowlands?"

"Nope." I never did. How seriously is Beck hurt?"

"About as bad as it gets. He's dying."

Frank wanted to yell, No! He can't die! Not like this. It isn't fair. He fought to regain self-control. "Are you sure?"

"That's what the doctors are saying. Hell, he took a shot in the gut, and another one close to the heart. It's a miracle that he made it to the hospital alive."

"Is he conscious?"

Cranville nodded down the hallway. A grim looking professional in green surgical attire was approaching. "We're about to find out."

The stranger introduced himself. "I'm Doctor Palomar. We took the bullet from Mr. Beck's abdomen. The other one was too close to his heart to risk removing it. All we bought him is a little time. Mr. Beck is awake. He's even alert. He's one of those rare individuals that comes out from under anesthesia almost immediately." He shook his head. "It might have been better for him if he hadn't. He's in a considerable amount of pain, and he can't last much longer."

Frank turned to Cranville. "I know I'm out of line, but hear me out. You have eyewitnesses to the shootings tonight. I doubt if Beck can add anything to make a real difference. Convicting Sheila Beck is a piece of cake. I have to talk to him. If he knows he's dying, maybe he'll tell the truth about Everett and Cleo Hale. I'm asking you to give me a few minutes with him. Just a few minutes," he pleaded.

Frank held his breath waiting for a response. So much hinged on Cranville's answer.

Cranville looked over at the doctor. "Can we talk to him?"

Palomar shrugged. "You can't hurt him, that's for sure. He's asking for a Detective Frank Damien. He asked me to call him. I have one of the nurses trying to locate him now." He wearily shrugged. "I don't think he'll make it here in time."

"This is your lucky day, Doctor," Cranville said caustically. He nodded at Frank. "This is Detective Frank Damien."

The shoe was on the other foot now, Frank realized, but he had no desire to take advantage of the upper hand that had just been dealt him. "A few minutes with him, Lieutenant. Then he's all yours. What do you say?"

Cranville tried to be good-natured about it. "Thanks. I would like to ask the son of a bitch why his wife wanted to waste him. I'll come in with you.

Doctor Palomar put out a restraining hand. "Mr. Beck wants to talk to Detective Damien alone."

Cranville shot Frank a sympathetic glance. "That's tough, Damien. Without a witness, any statement he makes is only hearsay."

Frank turned to the doctor. "There'll be a nurse in there?"

"I'm sorry. Mr. Beck was very explicit. He wants to see you alone. He asked that the room be cleared when and if you showed up." He shrugged. "The man is dying. He has a right to go out any way he wants to and with anyone he wants to."

Cranville cursed. "Do we have time to put a wire on Damien, Doctor?"

Palomar shook his head. "He could go anytime."

"Then what in the hell are we standing here for?" Frank asked impatiently.

Frank followed Doctor Palomar down the hall. The intensive care unit consisted of three beds. Only one of the beds was occupied. Outside, a few feet across from the area which was glassed, rather than walled in, two nurses periodically glanced at monitors, looking for signs of distress, or cardiac arrest.

Suddenly, Frank was alone in the room with Beck. Beck was hooked up to several pieces of machinery. A screen monitored his heart beats, the steady blips filling the room. His face was a sickly gray. His breathing was labored.

Death hovered like a hungry vulture.

Frank took a seat beside the bed. Beck whispered. "I'm in bad shape. No one is saying anything, but I can see it in their faces."

Frank nodded. "I won't lie to you, Beck. They say you're dying."

Beck coughed. He grimaced. "I knew I could count on you to tell me the truth. Guys like you always play it by the book."

"Then why not reciprocate? You killed Everett and Cleo Hale, didn't you?"

Beck coughed again. "Why do you think I called you in here? The moment Sheila pointed the gun at me and used it, I figured I was a goner. My time is getting short. I want to set the record straight." He tried to smile but it turned into a painful grimace. "I know I'm going to burn for killing Everett, but I didn't kill Cleo. Strange, isn't it? Man only worries about his soul when he's about to lose it." He sputtered. Blood appeared at the edge of his lips.

Frank looked out to the nurses' station. One of the nurses was already moving this way. "Let me get you a doctor," Frank offered.

The nurse entered the room. Beck whispered. "It's okay. Leave us alone." And when she didn't leave, he rasped. "I said leave us alone."

After the nurse reluctantly departed, Beck went on, "I said I didn't kill Cleo." Beck attempted another smile. The very effort caused him to cry out in pain. "You were the only one who cared about the truth, Damien. I guess that gives you, of all people, the right to hear it."

Beck coughed again. He clutched at his abdomen and sucked in his breath. "You're an annoying son of a bitch, Damien, but you're a good cop. You called it right. Cleo and I planned Everett's murder together. She waited until Everett was asleep, and then she called me. It was her idea to kill him. What does it matter whose idea it was now? I went along with killing Everett because I loved her. She wanted the insurance money. All I wanted was Cleo. You ever love a woman that much, Damien?" He paused. His eyes slowly closed. Frank was afraid he was dead. He looked up at the monitor. Beck's heartbeats, though now erratic, indicated he was still alive.

Beck gradually opened his eyes. "After I smashed Everett over the head with a hammer, and he was dead, it struck me like a bolt of lightening that we'd actually committed murder, and that we were never going to get away with it. I started to shake I was so scared. I was supposed to hit Cleo to make it appear that she was stunned by an intruder after he killed Everett. She'd already wet her hair and run water in the shower to make it look as if she was attacked after she got out of the shower. We were in the bathroom. I raised my hand to strike her as we planned, but I couldn't do it. She became angry. She said I was going to ruin everything. She began to slam blows to her own head with her fists."

Beck made a face. He clutched his stomach again. "Jesus, it hurts. Sheila got me in the gut, did you know that?"

Frank acknowledged that he did, impatient for Beck to continue. Beck could have hours or minutes or maybe only seconds.

"I grabbed Cleo's wrist. That's when I saw the diamond on her finger. She was supposed to throw it out with the jewelry that I was gong to bury in the cove at the end of the rocks on my way out of there." The pain of remembering mingled with his physical pain. "I responded angrily and tried to take it off her finger. She fought me. She screamed at me, telling me she'd earned the damn thing. She promised that no one would ever know she'd kept it, except the two of us. That she'd hide it where no one could ever find it. I told her the fucking ring would send us to the electric chair. She laughed. She seemed to be enjoying our confrontation. I became so angry, my hitting her was a reflex action. I hit her harder than I meant to. She fell to the floor, her head connecting with the edge of the sink. I called out her name. She was unconscious, but she was breathing, I swear it."

He gasped in pain. All I could think of, besides being afraid I'd hurt her, was that Cleo's plan was working after all, and we had to go through with it, or stand trial for murder. I ran outside. Using the walkway, I climbed down on the rocks. I could only go past the first row of boulders. The tide was up. I was a few houses down when I remembered the goddamn ring. I was afraid it would put a nail in both our coffins. I started to go back. I saw a figure in the window of the dimly-lit living room. I thought it was Cleo. My first feeling was one of relief. She was going to be all right. My next thought was that I didn't feel like another battle with her. I decided to trust her to conceal the ring until I could take it away from her later."

He gasped again and pointed at the glass of water with a straw sticking out of it. Frank passed it to him. It was obvious that time, like sand in an hour glass, was running out for Doug Beck.

"The next day, I heard that she was dead, horribly beaten. I didn't do that to her. Hell, I didn't even do that to Everett. When it was reported that she was found dead in the bed alongside Everett, I didn't know what to do. She was nowhere near the bed when I left. I couldn't go to the police. I was guilty of killing Everett, but I swear to you, I didn't kill Cleo."

"Why should I believe you? Why should I believe that a murder plot hatched up by you and Cleo went astray? Why kill Everett Hale? If you and Cleo had something going, why didn't she just divorce him?"

"The money from the insurance policy. I told you that. Anyway, Everett wouldn't consider divorce. Cleo was a status symbol for him. A perverse kind of reverse discrimination. You have to believe me. I have no reason to lie to you now. I'm dying."

"Assuming I choose to believe you, and you have to admit it's a little far fetched that someone would show up only minutes after you supposedly left to kill Cleo"

"What about the figure you say you saw in the window? Man or woman?"

Beck frowned. "I've thought about that a lot. Because I thought it was Cleo, I assumed it was a woman. Now, I don't know. Whoever it was had a key to the house and the combination to the gate. They must have come through the front of the house."

Frank sighed. "There were a lot of people with access to the house. You had a key, weekend tenants could have made a copy of the key, the family all had one, and God knows how many other people. Did Miramba have a key?"

"I think so, but you're right. Everett loved to show off. Cleo told me that he kept a drawer full of keys to the beach house. He would take one out and toss it to a client, or someone he wanted to impress, and say "Spend a few days at my beach house as my guest." It made him feel important."

"If you didn't kill Cleo, who else would have wanted her dead?"

Blood trickled down Beck's chin. He let out an agonized cry. "I've asked myself that question over and over again? Now, I've run out of time. I'm leaving it up to you to find out who killed her."

Beck paused to catch his breath. His eyelids fluttered. Frank glanced over at the heart monitor, thinking, stay alive, Beck, stay alive long enough to tell me everything.

His voice barely a whisper, Beck said, "You don't believe me, do you?"

Frank paced the floor at the foot of the bed. "I don't know what I believe." Frank returned to Beck's side.

Beck reached out for Frank's hand as if to hold on to life. "You have to believe me. We don't like each other, but in the end, it seems we have a lot in common. Who besides you and me cares as much as we do about finding Cleo's killer?" He wheezed, struggling for breath, then shuddered, and then he was still.

The monitor above him gave off an ominous tone. A solid line moved steadily across the screen. Palomar and two nurses rushed into the room. They pushed Frank aside.

Frank watched as an effort was made to revive Doug Beck, knowing all the while that the effort was futile.

He wandered outside the room. Cranville was waiting down the hall. Frank shook his head. "I'm sorry. I didn't get to ask him why Sheila Beck wanted to kill him." He rubbed a weary hand across his brow. "She got her wish. Beck's gone."

"Did you get what you came for?"

"Maybe more than I came for."

"What'll you do with the information?"

Frank shrugged. "I don't know yet. The truth has been a long time coming. I guess I'll deal with that before I do anything."

***

Before Frank could go home, there were two more stops he felt that he needed to make.

The first was to Miramba's room. She was under heavy guard to protect her from a hungry press corp. Frank showed his identification to the uniformed policeman at the door.

The cop responded, "Santa Barbara? You're a long way from home aren't you?"

Frank flushed angrily. " We can make this easy, officer, or we can do it the hard way. I just left Lieutenant Cranville. I was with Beck when he died a few moments ago." Frank continued his bluff. "Any more questions?"

The cop stepped aside, opened the door to Miramba's room and made way for Frank to enter.

It struck Frank that with all she'd been through this evening, a bullet wound, and surgery, she was still a beautiful sight. She lay flat on her back. Her eyes were closed.

Frank approached the bed. He had no idea how much time he had before someone would try to oust him from the room. He'd risked exposure and reprimand because he was counting on the fact that unlike Beck, she'd still be suffering from the after-effects of anesthesia. People drifting in and out of anesthesia seldom remembered all the visitors, much less what they said to them.

"Miramba?" He whispered, shaking her very gently.

She opened her eyes. "Damien!" She yawned. "Did you come to view the body? Sorry to disappoint you. I'm going to make it. The bullet went clear through me." She smiled. A gentler smile than held ever seen her deliver. "Only the good die young, Damien."

"Not always true. Beck is dead."

Miramba drew in her breath. Her dark eyes became pool of distress. "I was afraid of that. And, Sheila? What happened to Sheila?"

In his haste to talk to Beck and Miramba, Frank hadn't asked after Sheila Beck. "I don't know. I imagine she's in jail. There were enough witnesses to warrant her arrest. Why did she come gunning for you and Beck?"

"Something Doug said. He was trying to rile her. He wanted to get her out of his life." A frown passed across her lovely face. "He went too far."

"What did he say to her?"

"I don't know exactly. All he told me was that he'd given her reason to leave him. Something about another woman. I'm sure it never occurred to him that he'd given her reason to kill him. You don't care about Doug, or me. Why are you...why are you here?" Her voice trailed sleepily.

He nudged her awake. She stared at him in confusion.

"Beck confessed to killing Everett Hale," Frank said.

"I don't believe you."

"That he would tell me? Or that he killed him? I think you've always known he killed Everett Hale. Then there's Cleo? Did he kill her, too, or was he telling the truth about her being alive when he left the beach house that night? Are you the one who made it a double homicide?"

"Fuck you, Damien. I don't have a clue what you're hinting at." She yawned. "I'm tired. Get the hell out of here."

She reached for the cord that would summon a nurse. Frank placed his hand over the button before she could press it. "Don't bother. I'm leaving."

***

Cranville was still in the building. He didn't look too pleased to see Frank again. "Are you still here? What's the matter? Didn't you get everything you wanted? I just heard that you finessed your way into Miramba's room. You're out of line, Damien, and you're out of your jurisdiction."

Frank nodded. "I apologize, Lieutenant. I'm on my way out . What's happening with Sheila Beck? You booked her, of course."

"Sure, but a lot of good that does us. Last I heard she was on her way to the psycho ward. After she opened fire on Miramba and Beck, she dropped the gun, turned to one of the guests at the party and said, "He used me. He deserves to die. That's the last words she spoke."

"Her lawyer told her to clam up?"

"Not that simple. She freaked out. She's catatonic."

"Shock?"

Cranville shrugged. "Maybe. The shrinks say she may never come out of it. She has a history of being unstable."

"In a way I feel somewhat responsible. I pushed her hard after Beck was released from custody."

"You didn't pull the trigger, Damien."

"I know. In a way, Beck did that all himself. If I can be of any help, Cranville, let me know."

Cranville raised his hands in protest. "Please, Damien, spare me that. Just get the hell out of here and let me do my job."

Frank felt for him. Cranville's predicament was a familiar one. The lieutenant had an open and shut case. A shooting with dozens of witnesses, and he had a murderer who would probably never stand trial.

It was both the best and the worst way for a homicide investigation to end.

***

Bart Crossman wasn't happy about being rousted out of bed at 2:30 a.m. He ran his hands through his hair, tied the sash of his robe tighter around his waist, and glared at Frank. "Damien! What the hell!"

Frank shifted uneasily. He should have waited until morning. "Just a few minutes of your time, Bart. Can I come in?"

The D.A.'s wife appeared at his side. Bart, who is it?"

"A detective, Jill. Go back to sleep."

She yawned. "Too late for that. Ask the man in. I'll make you both some coffee."

Frank gave Jill Crossman a grateful smile. "Thanks, Mrs. Crossman. I'm sorry for disturbing you at this ungodly hour. I wouldn't have, if my business wasn't important."

She smiled. "It's okay. When I first met Bart I was engaged to marry a gynecologist. I wasn't too happy about the fact that baby doctors are pulled out of bed in the middle of the night. So, I married me a lawyer. Serves me right."

Crossman gave his wife an irritated glance. "I thought you were going to make us some coffee." He led Frank to the living room. He flipped on a light switch and motioned Frank to the closest chair.

"Your wife is a good sport," Frank said. "I like her."

Crossman responded sharply. "What in the hell brings you to my home at this hour?"

"You heard about Beck?"

Crossman threw himself down in a chair across from Frank. He reached for a pack of cigarettes on a small table beside it. "I heard that his wife shot him. When I went to bed…" He scowled. "Some of us do sleep, you know, Beck was critical. Is this what this is all about? A news bulletin? Jesus, Frank!"

"Beck is dead."

"Pardon me for not getting too excited about that piece of news, or seem to be grief-stricken. So, he's dead. So what?"

Frank stood. He paced the floor. "I talked to him right before he died."

Crossman flipped the ash off his cigarette, missing the glass ashtray. "The hell you say!"

"He was asking for me."

Crossman was wide awake now. "Why?"

"Guilty conscience, I guess. He knew he was dying. He confessed to killing Everett Hale, but he swears he didn't kill Cleo. Oh, I know it sounds crazy, but he said that Cleo Hale was alive when he left the beach house. That by itself should give us reason to re-open the case."

He looked for signs of encouragement from Crossman, but none came.

"Say something Bart."

"Okay, but you're not going to like it. There's a murdering punk sitting in jail where he belongs, with the death penalty hanging over his head. Cassady mutilated a man, a woman, and a child. They're about to bring in a guilty verdict. If you go off half-cocked blabbing about Beck's dying confession, Cassady's attorney will call for a dismissal, and maybe even end up with an acquittal. Are you forgetting that Cassady is considered guilty of the Hale murders by a large majority of people? Cast doubt on that fact, and the son of a bitch might walk away from the other murders. Is that what you want? I sure as hell don't. We don't always win, Frank. Cassady could be a win. Don't turn it into a loss."

"You want me to keep my mouth shut about Beck's confession!"

Crossman nodded.

"You supposedly stand for justice! Beck has to be exposed, as well as a system that allows guilty men to go free," Frank protested. "Someone is getting away with murder."

"Your uncorroborated version, Frank, and only if I'm supposed to believe that you believe Beck wasn't lying about not killing Cleo Hale. You've been perfectly willing to brand him a liar until now. I'm not convinced there was another person at the beach house. Think about it,

Frank. It's a security gated colony, yet you'd have me believing that the house at the beach was like Grand Central Station that night."

Frank sank down in the char. "If we do nothing, what in the hell is it all about?"

"It's about justice, Frank. Beck is dead. Just how much justice to you want? He was tried and found guilty by a higher court than ours. For God's sake," Crossman pleaded. "Don't give Cassady a way to go free."

Jill Crossman came into the room. She carried two mugs of coffee. She handed one to her husband. She offered the other one to Frank.

Frank shook his head. "No, thanks. I have to be going. Marian's waiting up for me."

Crossman placed his coffee on the table. "What are you going to do Frank?"

"I told you. I'm going home."

"Then what?"

Frank stared at his feet. There were times he hated not only his job but all the people connected with it. Tonight was one of those nights. "I won't fuck up the case against Cassady, don't worry."

Crossman let out a sigh of relief. "You won't regret it Frank, when you've had time to think about it."

"I already do." He nodded to Jill Crossman's direction. "Thanks for the coffee. Sorry I can't stay to drink it."

"I was thinking, Frank," Crossman said, "How come you never stopped to ask yourself why Beck chose you to bare his soul to? After all, you were the one that hounded him. You made his life miserable."

"Maybe, because like he said, I'm the only one who's interested in the truth." Frank shrugged. "I guess that was established here tonight."

Frank let himself out. Jill Crossman moved to her husband's side. She gave him a sympathetic glance.

"You heard?" He asked.

"Enough." She stared in the direction of the door that Frank had just closed behind him. "I was thinking how hard it must be for Frank Damien to do what you asked." She patted his hand. "Let's go back to bed."

Crossman gently kissed her. He turned out the light in the living room and took her by the hand. He followed her up the stairs to bed.

Crossman lay awake long after he heard his wife's steady breathing indicating that she was asleep. There would be precious little sleep for him tonight. He hated what he'd had to do to Frank Damien. This was one time when the good guys just couldn't win.

CHAPTER 13

Although the weather was unusually humid, Frank knew that his sweat-stained suit had nothing to do with the climate. It was as if time had stood still. Once again a case he should have been able to solve was out of control, mandated by events, and not by him.

Cordova had been in custody, hopelessly insane, so the experts were saying. Cordova's sanity, or lack of it, was of little consequence to Frank. What was of consequence was that he'd been paid to protect the people of New York City, and he'd failed them. Because he had, a number of women had died. He had never stopped blaming himself for his inability to see through Cordova's cool façade much sooner. And he'd never stopped thrashing himself for not being a better cop.

More importantly, and of much more significance, was the fact that he'd never been able to forgive himself for Claire's ordeal.

From the onset, the Hale killings had been troublesome to him. More than they should have been because Frank had been afraid to confront his fear of losing control. Losing control was something he hadn't allowed himself to do all those years ago.

As he neared his apartment, Frank wiped sweat from his brow. Maybe this time things would be different. The last time he'd felt this way he'd had no one to share his troubled thoughts with. Not even Claire. She'd been through so much she hadn't needed the burden of his own nagging guilt.

Marian was curled up on the couch, asleep. Frank bent down to kiss her on the cheek. She rubbed her eyes. "What time is it?"

"It's after three. You shouldn't have waited up for me."

She rubbed the back of her neck. "I dozed off. A nurse from the hospital called here looking for you. She said Doug Beck was asking after you, but that was hours ago. I told her I thought you were on your way to the hospital. What did he want with you?"

"To confess." His tone was flat. "Before he died, he admitted to killing your ex-husband."

"He's dead? And he confessed? Then he really did kill Ev?" Disturbance filled her eyes. "If he confessed to killing Ev, I'd think you'd be relieved, but you look...you look strange. Isn't this what you wanted? To have solid proof you were right about him? What else did he say?"

"He said we had a lot in common?"

"What does that mean?"

"Wanting the truth, I guess. He died before he could expand on it. You're making my going after Beck sound like a vendetta. All I wanted was the truth. Killing Everett was the only crime Beck confessed to. He claimed he didn't kill Cleo."

She frowned. "How can that be possible? Unless..." Her eyes widened. "You always thought whoever killed Ev and Cleo wasn't alone. Was there someone with Doug Beck at the beach house that night?"

Frank fell into a chair across from the couch. "He says not."

"Then how...?"

"I don't know." He took a seat beside her on the couch. He placed his hands on her shoulders to get her full attention. "Listen to me, Marian. I want to tell you something I've never told a living soul."

"Something to do with Ev's murder?"

He moved his hands from her shoulder and took her hand in his. "No. It's about me and Cordova. I didn't tell you everything. Nor did I tell you the real reason I felt it necessary to leave New York."

She noted the moisture glistening on Frank's forehead. She wiped his brow with her fingertips. "Are you all right, Frank?"

He brushed her hand away. "No. I'm not. That's what I'm trying to tell you. After Cordova was put away, I underwent my own identity crisis. I was terrified that the Department would find out that I was cracking up. My work was the only thing Cordova had left me. I couldn't let them take it away from me. I knew even then, that Claire was lost to me." He sighed heavily. "I became one of the walking wounded. I hid the fact that I was approaching near mental collapse. When Claire left me, and I was afraid I couldn't hide my condition any longer, I quit and came here to Santa Barbara. I needed to work. To continue being a cop if at all possible. I couldn't do it in New York. Not any more."

She gave him an anxious look. "And Ev's murder? What does this have to do with what happened in New York?"

He gently kissed her. " From the very beginning, from the first moment I saw Everett and Cleo Hale caked with their own blood, I felt uneasy. Their deaths opened up wounds I'd convinced myself were healed. I think it had to do with the violent way they died, and the psychological implications. The fact that someone had moved Cleo's body and set the stage. For what reason? It was as if Cordova was reaching out to pull me under." He shrugged. "It was inevitable, I suppose, that somebody, someday, would make me take a good look at myself and my hang-ups."

"Why didn't you get help in New York? What you were feeling was nothing to be ashamed of."

"I wasn't ashamed. I was afraid they'd take my badge. If they had, there wouldn't have been a police force in this country that would have taken me on."

"Oh, Frank. The little I've learned about the police force since I've known you, tells me they wouldn't have tossed you aside. You were, are," she stressed, "too good a cop."

"Am I?" He took his hands off her shoulders and raised them. They were shaking. "Look at me!"

She clutched his hands in her own. "My God, Frank. I didn't know, and I should have. I've been blinded by the fact that these last few months together have been so special for us. In the light of Doug Beck's confession, it isn't easy to ask you to back off, especially if what he said about not killing Cleo is really true." She bit down on her lip. "I'm just not sure what a renewed commitment on your part to pursue this thing will do to us, to you. I'm afraid, Frank. You're teetering on the edge, and I'm concerned that further involvement will bring about a breakdown you can't hide or control this time around." She sighed. " I love you, and you have to deal with this in your own way. I won't fight you, or complicate matters by trying to tell you what to do."

"Thanks. It's not just your decision nor mine." Frank told her about the D.A.'s wish to sweep Beck's dying statement under the rug.

"No wonder you're angry," she responded. "I won't lie to you and tell you that I'm not relieved. All I've wanted since the night Ev died is for the tragedy of it to go away. I never tried to hide that from you. Don't fight Crossman, Frank," she pleaded. "And don't fight me. Let it be over. I'm tired of dealing with it, Frank, and I'm tired of worrying about what it's going to do to us."

Frank felt like he was drowning and no one was throwing him a life jacket. Marian seemed so remote, unreachable, despite her willingness not to thwart him. He rose. "It's been a rough night. I think we both need some sleep. I'll take you home."

He waited for her to say she'd stay the night. It would be the first, and the best time for her to make the gesture.

Instead, she gathered up her purse and headed for the door.

***

It was difficult at first to see in the dimly lighted room. When his eyes adjusted, Frank made out two figures, one standing, the other slouched against the wall. The man was smiling down at the weeping woman. Blood dripped from the knife in his hand. Red blotches stained her stomach, and her legs.

The woman looked up and mouthed a scream that never left her throat. Her eyes moved accusingly in Frank's direction.

The woman was Claire.

Another woman appeared. She made as if to comfort Claire. Cordova lifted the knife and aimed it at the woman's throat. The woman smiled. First at Frank, then over at Cordova.

Cordova's knife touched the other woman's throat. Her smile was replaced by a shrill scream. Her green eyes sparkled angrily. Frank watched helplessly as the knife embedded itself in her neck.

The second woman in the room was Marian.

Frank shot up in bed. Another nightmare! Worse than all the others.

He looked down at his sweat stained pajamas. He slipped out of the bed and made his way to the bathroom.

Frank looked at his image in the mirrored wall. You're thirty-eight, and you look ten years older. He thought about what Marian had said about his being on the edge. You look like a man about to go over the edge, he allowed. He gripped the sink as if to hold onto sanity.

He turned on the shower and stepped inside the glassed enclosure. Hot water ran down his body washing away the sweat, but not the effects of the dream.

When he stepped back into the bedroom the phone beside the bed was ringing urgently. Frank picked up the receiver, nodded a few times, said, "I'll take care of it," and placed the receiver back on its hook.

He had barely hung up when the phone rang again. This time it was Marian.

"Are you okay, Frank?"

"Yeah, I'm fine. I have to go back to the hospital. Miramba called the station. She wants to see me."

There was silence on the other end of the line. "It isn't going to go away, is it?'

Frank sat on the edge of the bed. "I want it to. I didn't call Miramba. She called me."

"You could ignore the call."

And always wonder why she called me in the first place, he thought. "I have to go. We'll talk later. I'll call you…"

But she had hung up on him.

Frank made it past the dense security that both the hospital and Miramba had employed.

Miramba was sitting up in bed when he entered the room. The hospital garb had been replaced by an apricot negligee with a plunging neckline. There were flowers on the tables, the window sill, and on the floor. She should have been overshadowed by the profuse array. Instead, she dominated the room.

Miramba waved at the floral splendor. "My fans and friends. It's nice to know that people care."

Frank moved to the only piece of furniture in the room that wasn't occupied with flowers, a chair by the bed. He sat down. "You called me?"

Miramba sighed. "It would have been nice if you'd asked me how in the hell I feel."

"No need. You seem to be in rare form." He glanced down at his watch. I have things to do, so if you'd...

"Come to the point?" She shrugged. "Have it your way. I had this ridiculous dream last night. I dreamed that you came to my room and you'd seen Doug right before he died. I dreamed that you accused me of killing my own sister. Then, this morning, I found out your being here was no dream after all."

"I was here last night. I don't deny it."

"I want to know what happened when you spoke to Doug, and why you'd accuse me of doing such a horrible thing."

Frank gave her an appraising glance. There wasn't a jury in the world who would convict her of anything. "Beck confessed to killing Everett Hale. He denied killing your sister. He said he saw someone in the beach house as he was leaving by way of the rocks."

"You believed him?"

"Dying men seldom lie. They're afraid they'll go to hell. You don't seem surprised that he confessed to killing Hale."

She played with the ribbon nestled in her cleavage. "I suppose not. I guess I always knew it was possible he killed them."

"Is that why you hired a high-powered attorney? To protect a killer? Or did you hire Schmidt to keep your own ass out of the line of fire?"

"You don't give up easily, do you? I didn't kill Cleo, Damien. Not for myself, and not for Doug. The very idea is preposterous."

"Who do you think did?"

She gave him a black-eyed stare. "You might try Sheila."

"How would she have managed it? She only arrived in this country that night. How could she have known where to find Beck and Cleo?"

"When Doug left the party he started for home. Within a block of his apartment he changed his mind, or so he said. Sheila could have seen him and followed him to the beach house. Believe me, she's capable of it."

"Why would she do that?"

"She was insanely jealous. She claimed to have come here to take Doug's son away from him. I think she came here to make a last and desperate play for Doug."

"They'd been separated for a long time. It was supposedly her idea to return to England."

Miramba laughed. "Doug's one rare show of chivalry. He didn't want anyone to know he sent her away. Sheila left here kicking and screaming. She called him at least twice a week. He finally agreed that she could visit him once a year, for the kid's sake, and to get her off his back."

"You think she hated Cleo enough to kill her?"

"She hated anyone who got close to Doug." Miramba tossed back the sheet, pulled up her negligee, and pointed at her bandaged side. "Look what she did to me."

Frank rose from the chair. "I'll think about what you've said." He smiled, but the expression didn't reach his eyes. "I suppose you know that Sheila Beck is catatonic."

She shook her head. "No." She smiled. "You don't believe me, do you? You think I fed Sheila to you because she can't defend herself."

"The thought crossed my mind." Just as the thought had crossed his mind before he'd entered the room that Sheila might have been the shadowy figure in the window that Beck had seen. He didn't tell Miramba that.

He was on his way out of the room when he looked back at her. "By the way. Were you in love with Doug Beck?"

She laughed. The sound filled the room. "Really, Damien! Do I look like a woman who's grieving for a lost love?"

Frank stared into black taunting eyes.

As he pulled the door to, he was aware of the clammy condition of his hands, and the beads of sweat gathering on his brow.

Lieutenant Larry Cranville wasn't overjoyed to see Frank. He looked up from his paper-laden desk. "What do you want now, Damien?"

"I want to see Sheila Beck."

"What for?"

Frank remembered Crossman's warning. "Maybe I can help you out. I might be able to get through to her. There were moments during the Hale murder investigation when I believed that she wanted to trust me."

"Her attorney would have a fit."

"He doesn't have to know."

Cranville leaned back in his chair. "Coming from you that's a surprise. I would have sworn you played it by the book."

"I've broken a few rules, but then we all do. How about it, Cranville?"

Cranville shook his head. He picked up the phone and barked an order at someone on the other end. "She's in the County psychiatric ward. I don't think you'll get anything out of her." He shrugged. "You sure as hell can't make things any worse."

***

Sheila Beck sat in a chair by the window. She was alone in the room. A white-coated attendant and a uniformed policeman waited outside.

She stared ahead of her, her eyes focused on the wall beyond. Frank swallowed. She was pathetically beautiful, almost ethereal, like an elusive shadow.

Beck pulled a chair close to her. He cleared his throat. "I don't know if you can hear me, Sheila. I'm going to take a chance that you can. I talked to your husband right before he died. He killed Hale. I think he told you that, just like you said he did. Now, Cleo? That's another story. Did you follow Beck to the beach house and kill Cleo Hale?"

Beck glanced out the window. Three stories below the world was carrying on a normal existence. "What in the hell did Beck say to you to make you angry enough to want to kill him? Did he throw his affair with Miramba in your face, rub your nose in it so you had to react?"

Frank positioned himself directly in her line of vision. "I, too, have known how it feels to love someone who no longer wants you around. It hurts like hell." He looked away and spoke more to himself than to her. "I've known how it feels to lose your grip, but I held on. I came back to fight for a better life. Or if not better, one I could handle."

He addressed her again. "You have a son, Sheila. He needs you. You can beat a first degree murder rap with a diminished capacity plea. As for Cleo Hale, the case is closed. Not my idea, the D.A.'s. Beck paid a heavy price for his part in it. If you were there, no one has to know it except you and me."

Sheila Beck stared sightlessly ahead of her. Frank threw up his hands. "Don't you see? You will have gotten away with it. No one wants to pursue this case any more. Beat this murder charge and you can start your life all over again. Beck isn't worth dying for, or burying yourself in a living hell."

Frank took her hand. It was limp and unresponsive. "You said Beck used you. How? Did he push you into killing Cleo?"

Frank strode to the window. "There's a world out there just waiting for you to live it. You can do that, or you can vegetate. Your choice. At the worst, you'll only do a few years."

He sighed. "Looking at you, I realize that it could be me sitting there. I won't let it happen." He raised his hands. They were clammy, but steady. "I have a chance at a new life, and I'm going to take it."

He moved to the door. He was never sure what possessed him to say, "I was the last man to see and talk to your husband. He didn't blame you for anything. He loved you."

She didn't stir, but a tear rolled down her cheek.

He was glad he had lied to her.

Marian was in the downstairs shop when he arrived at the house on Chapparral. She looked up in surprise and excused herself as she moved away from the customer she was waiting on.

There was an anxious look in her eyes. "I'm sorry I hung up on you, Frank. I'm sorry..."

He placed his fingers on her lips. "Don't be sorry, I had it coming."

She tilted her head to one side. "There's something different about you. What happened with Miramba?"

"Nothing important."

"You're smiling. What really happened?"

"Freedom happened. I'm through with the Hale murder case. All I want to do is now is to concentrate on us. I want to go back to New York. I belong there. I want you to come with me."

"This is so sudden. New York?"

How can I explain, he thought, that being with Sheila Beck was a warning signal. A portent of my own future unless I do something about it. Now, before it's too late. Facing up to his past was part of that process.

"Would you at least think about going to New York with me?" he asked.

She smiled. "I'll think about nothing else. Now get out of here and let me get back to work."

Two days later his resolve to put the Hale case behind him was shattered by a phone call from Sarah Meadows, the woman who lived next door to the Hale beach house.

Someone was camping out next door. Since it could be Derek, Frank had no choice but to follow up on the call.

CHAPTER 14

Tom Lawson handed Frank a cigarette. Frank accepted it, keeping his eyes on the road ahead. He'd asked Tom along today because up till now he'd been the only police contact the old woman had encountered on the Hale case. When they arrived at the beach colony, Frank left Tom with Sarah Meadows while he went inside the Hale beach house.

The FOR SALE sign was faded and weather-beaten. Marian had had offers on the house, but none that even came close to covering the staggering mortgages Everett Hale had placed on it, so she'd reluctantly held onto it. Failing a miracle, her ability to keep it would come to an end when the bank took the house back in less than ninety days.

The place looked much the same as Frank remembered it, and yet significantly different. All the original furniture remained, even the bed where they'd found Everett and Cleo Hale dead. The Crime Lab had stripped the bed, and new linen and a quilted bedspread now covered the king-sized four-poster.

The transformation would be Marian's handiwork, Frank guessed. She liked neatness and order. She'd understandably fixed up the room to make the house more saleable: a desperate attempt to give the illusion nothing horrible had happened here.

But it had. And no amount of decorating was ever going to change it. The other bedrooms looked untouched and unlived in. Frank returned to the master bedroom. He touched the top of the bed, and the quilted bedspread. Neatly made, but somehow imperfect. Marian would have made a perfect bed. Unbidden, a chill ran through him. The hair on the back of his neck stood up. Someone had slept here, and recently. Someone with a sense of the macabre. Why sleep here when there were two other bedrooms in the house?

Frank moved to the bathroom. Cleo had been killed in here. Yet, the morning they'd found the bodies this room had looked as unlived in as a hotel room. This room, too, had been used recently. The sink no longer glistened. There was a film on the tub and on the sink. Two, instead of three rows of orderly towels were now stacked on the wall unit.

Frank left the bedroom and went into the kitchen. Here too, there was subtle evidence that someone had been here recently. The intruder had tried to cover his or her tracks, and, whoever it was might have gotten away with it if they'd been dealing with an untrained eye.

Derek!

Tom came in through the open sliding doors that led to the sandy expanse and to the rocks below. "The old lady says she never saw who it was, but she swears someone has been here." He shook his head. "The woman is driving me crazy. Hell, Frank, the house is on the market. Lots of people have been here. My sister's in the real estate business. She says she's shown houses as late as ten-o-clock at night, and they touch everything. I'd bet money that's the real explanation for the old woman's fantasies about an intruder."

Frank stroked his chin. "Sarah Meadows isn't crazy, Tom. Someone has been here besides potential buyers for the house. Someone who's stayed the night, or at least bunked out here for a few hours."

"You think it was the Hale kid?"

Frank smiled. In a few years Tom would be a top-notch cop. If he stayed around that long, that is. Burn-out in this job was an occupational hazard. Then again, this wasn't New York, and murder wasn't on the menu every day in this neck of the woods.

"Could be," Frank said.

Tom grinned. "Where's the famous Damien hunch? Is it the kid, or isn't it, Frank?"

Frank's feelings for Marian were getting in the way. If it was Derek his being here would only complicate their lives. After a brief inner struggle, the cop in him won out. "I'd say it was a safe bet that it was Derek. What else did the old lady have to say?"

Tom sighed. "Same old stuff. Maybe you ought to talk to her, Frank. I could have missed something. I don't have your years of experience."

No, he didn't. Frank felt a twinge of guilt. He'd acted irresponsibly by not talking to Sarah Meadows, and by pawning her off onto Tom. She very well could have said something significant, that Tom, with his limited experience could have missed. Then again, she could just be a troublesome busybody. He sighed. Better check her out for himself. "Okay, I'll talk to her. Call for prints. Wait for them to get here. I'll be next door with Sarah Meadows."

Sarah Meadows was a small woman. She reminded Frank of an inquisitive little bird. Even her perfectly coiffed silver-grey hair ended in a peak like a bird's crop. Her beady brown eyes completed the picture. A widow for forty of her sixty-five years, Sarah Meadows had lived her life through others for so long it had become a habit.

Photographs filled the wall of her living room and adorned the top of a baby grand piano. Pictures of herself and a young man, her late husband, pictures of her sisters, brothers, nieces and nephews. It was a telltale glimpse into a life where the owner of these photographs lived on the outside looking in.

Frank looked from the woman to the huge glass picture windows that gave her a panoramic vista of the sand beyond and a blue-green ocean. If there was anything going on out there, she'd have to be blind to miss it. He doubted she missed much.

Sarah Meadows placed a steel rimmed spectacles on the bridge of her slender beak-like nose. "There, that's better. Now I can see what you look like. The young man told me you might be over to see me. He admires you, you know, but you tend to intimidate him." She sniffed. "Can't see why. You look nice enough to me. Some tea, or coffee, or lemonade?"

"Coffee would be nice."

She smiled. Company was all too few and far between. "Wonderful. Just give me a minute. I have some coffee brewing."

She returned a few moments later with a silver coffee pot, sugar bowl and creamer and two dainty cups and saucers on a tray.

"I'll join you if you don't mind." She filled two cups with the steaming liquid.

Frank took a sip. "We've looked over the house next door, Mrs. Meadows, and I think you're right. Someone has been spending time there recently. Did you see anyone specifically?"

She gave him a rueful smile. "Not really." She pursed her lips. "In fact, not at all, but I knew someone had been there."

"How did you know that?"

She moved to a chest and took out a key. "Instinct, Detective. Mrs. Hale gave me a key. To keep an eye on the place, you know. Lord knows how many keys her husband gave out. I thought I heard something over there, so I used my key." She gave him a smug look. "I may be an old woman, but I haven't lost my facilities. I sensed a recent presence. Since you've confirmed my suspicions, I'm glad I called you."

"Could it have been Derek Hale, Mrs. Meadows"

"It could have been, or it could have been one of those nasty creatures who live on the beach. When my late husband and I bought this house there were only three other houses along this strip. Things were different then. People didn't live on the streets and on the beach." Her look was disapproving.

No wonder Tom had passed her to him, Frank thought. Since he was here, best to make it count for something if he could. "I hate to go over old ground, Mrs. Meadows, but on the night of the murders, can you think of anything that you might have overlooked telling Tom about? Anything, no matter how small a detail."

She drew her brows together in a frown. "Don't think I haven't thought about it a million times. I had a headache that night and I'd taken one of my migraine pills. I retired early. I'm a light sleeper," she hastened to add. "If there had been a ruckus that night, I'd have heard it."

"You didn't see anyone outside the Hale beach house? Not Doug Beck, or anyone else?"

A look of disapproval filled her face. "You mean the man they arrested for the murders?" She leaned close. "Did he do it?"

"Yes, as a matter of fact, he did."

Her eyes widened. "Really! I heard that his wife shot him dead. The Lord works in mysterious ways." She pursed her lips piously.

Damned mysterious, Frank wanted to add, but considered that she would deem the statement blasphemous. "He sure does, Ma'am. So you never saw him that night?"

There was regret in her tone. "No. I only saw him once, just like I told your young associate. Just once, out on the patio with Mrs. Hale. To think, he was carrying on with her and him married all the time!"

Frank didn't want to give her fuel for idle gossip, and it had been too much to hope for that she would add anything of real importance at this late date. He handed her his business card. "Well, thanks for your help. If you think of anything relevant about that night, or if you see anyone hanging around the house next door, please call me. Especially call me if you see Derek Hale in the vicinity."

"Is the boy in trouble?"

Up to his neck, Frank thought. Out loud, he said. "I'd just like to talk to him. His mother would like to know he's all right."

"Nice woman that. Not real sociable, but a lady. Mr. Hale let her use the house after the divorce, but she didn't abuse the privilege. I can count the times on both hands that she came here. The same people who clean my house also clean the house next door." She massaged her knuckles. "I cleaned my own house for years till arthritis made it too painful. The cleaning people talk a lot, you know, gossip mostly. They said Mrs. Hale always left the place real nice. Hale's new wife, on the other hand, was a terrible housekeeper, so they say. Left towels all over the bathroom floor and never once put up a new set for those who came after her." She sniffed. "There were a lot of them, I tell you. She was some sort of entertainer, so they say." Her tone was disapproving.

She folded her arms across her bosom, a woman with purpose. "Rest assured, young man that I'll keep my eyes open." She gave him a bemused look. "I know it sounds awful, but I confess that I miss the activity next door, in spite of the rather crude goings on there."

Frank smiled. He didn't doubt the truth of her statement. The Hale murders had ended her main source of entertainment and left a terrible void in her life.

***

Frank would have rather eaten lead than talk to Marian right now. Putting it off wasn't gong to make it any easier for either of them.

She made it worse by opening the door of the house on Chapparral to him and flying into his arms. Her eyes sparkled. "I've been trying to reach you all day. The answer is yes, Frank. I'll go to New York with you."

He gently pushed her away. "New York will have to wait."

He led her to what had once been a parlor, and was now a cozy living room. He sat her down in a chair. He remained standing. "Someone has been staying at the beach house, Marian. We lifted some prints. Some of them belong to Derek. I've had a twenty-four watch placed on the house. If it is him, we'll get him."

She frowned. "Get him? That sounds ominous. Derek is a runaway, Frank, not a fugitive."

That depends on what or whose point of view you're coming from, Frank thought, "You want him found, don't you?" he said, skillfully skirting the real issue.

"Of course I want him found. I just don't want him hunted." She gave him a hard searching look. "How long is New York on hold for, Frank? Until we find Derek, or until you really get Ev's murder out of your system?"

She knew him far too well. "I won't lie to you, Marian. I don't know the answer to that question."

"You knew it when you asked me to go to New York with you."

That seems like a lifetime ago, Frank thought. Now, they seemed like two other people. Looking at Marian in this moment, and the way she looked back at him, he knew that their relationship had taken a giant step backward, and he was powerless to stop it. "I have to see it through, Marian. I thought I didn't, but now I know I have to."

"Then we have nothing further to say to each other, Frank. You can't know how sorry I am about that."

He knew only too well. All he had to do was take her own feelings and double them, and he had his own.

***

Derek had still to be found, and Frank had yet to see Marian since their last bitter encounter. He kept looking for an excuse to call her.

When it came, it was one of the worst days of Frank's life.

***

Frank was on his way out the door to lunch when Markham called him into his office.

"Sit down, Frank," he ordered.

Markham's usual genial demeanor was missing. Uneasiness swept over Frank. Whatever the man had to say, he knew he wasn't going to want to hear it.

Markham shook his head. "I guess there's no easy way to do this, Frank. Derek Hale is dead."

Frank shot forward in his chair. "What."

Markham sighed. "He's dead, Frank."

"How? When? Why?"

Markham weighed his next words carefully. He knew full well the potential volatility of the man who sat before him. Worse, he knew how Frank felt about Marian Hale. "One of our cars spotted the boy down by the old beach road between here and Ventura. They tried to take him easy, but something went wrong. The boy took off like a scared rabbit. One of the officers interpreted his panic for full flight. He called for back-up. The two cars managed to trap him. Derek Hale threw himself onto the rocks. He broke his neck. He died instantly, if that helps."

Frank squinted, shaking his head as if to clear it. He remembered Marian saying she didn't want Derek hunted. He had been hunted, and now he was dead. "Who gave orders to spook the kid? Why wasn't I called when they spotted him?"

"I told you, there was a foul-up."

"A foul-up! A boy is dead because two of our patrol cars played like it was Al Capone they were after. No, it doesn't help a bit that he died instantly. Derek may have been the only one left who can tell us what the hell went on at the beach house after Beck left it that night."

Markham reached for a manila envelope. He shook the contents of the envelope into the top of his desk. "We found these things on the Hale kid."

His head spinning, Frank fingered the objects. Four dollars and change. A wallet with pictures of his mother and sister. A key, and a folded piece of paper that when opened revealed several names and addresses. The beach house address, Jed Hale's apartment house, Doug Beck's office and home, and Miramba's address. There were check marks against all of them except Miramba's address.

Frank leaned back in his chair. "What was the little bastard doing? Playing detective or..."

"Blackmail?" Markham supplied. "How do you want to handle this, Frank? You want to tell Marian Hale, or do you want me to do it?"

Frank's voice was distant. "You do it. I can't face her right now. I feel responsible for Derek's death."

"That's ridiculous."

Frank's eyes shot daggers. "Don't let me off the hook, Captain, I'm not sure I deserve it."

Markham started to say something, but the dark look on Frank's face stopped him. He shrugged. "All right. I'll tell her. What will you be doing?"

"Checking the one place Derek may not have had a chance to. I'm going to see Miramba."

***

Miramba's Beverly Hills home was, like everything else she owned, a tribute to her beauty and a boost to her ego. Platinum and gold albums and posters from her two movies occupied the wall of the gold-leafed hallway that led to the solarium where Miramba waited for him.

Looking at her reclining on a leopard skin covered chaise like a carefully posed model in a magazine layout, Frank wondered if she ever let the kinks show, and immediately doubted it. She wore a long silver gown with a slit that reached her thighs, showcasing incredible legs. A Doberman and an Afghan Hound lay at her feet. The Doberman showed his teeth. The Afghan looked disinterested.

Frank gave the Doberman a wary glance. Miramba smiled. "Please, make yourself comfortable. Don't mind Charlie, he won't hurt you unless I tell him to." She reached down and petted the dog.

He took a seat, his eyes still focused on Charlie. Frank had a healthy respect for all dogs, but a special respect for Dobermans and German Shepherds.

Miramba sighed, a sound she managed to lace with sexual overtones. "What is it this time, Damien?"

"Derek Hale. Have you talked to him lately?"

She shuddered. "That little creep! Why would I talk to him?"

"We found a list of names and addresses on him. Your name and address was on that list."

She arched her eyebrows and yawned prettily. "Really! Why don't you ask him why he had my name on a list? And how he came by my address, incidentally. I don't exactly publicize it."

"I can't ask him anything. Derek Hale is dead."

She shifted position. There was no pretense of remorse. "I see. That must make it hard for you and whatshername. Marian, isn't it? How did he die? Not foul play, I hope. Of course it was foul play. Otherwise, why would you be here?"

Frank shook his head. "Not this time. Derek's death was an accident. Why would he want to see you, Miramba? There was no love lost between you two, was there?"

"Not an ounce. I have no idea why he wanted to see me." She grinned. "But I bet you have a theory or two. Don't keep me in suspense. Please, take center stage."

Funny she would use those words when he was so sure life was a stage for her. "I think Derek might have been playing detective." He paused. "Or, he might have been trying to blackmail you."

"Blackmail! For what? My life is an open book."

"Is it? There's your penchant for young men...and women. There's your hastily annulled marriage to a minor, and, finally, there's the possibility that you killed your sister."

He sat back, folded his arms and waited for her to respond.

Her eyes flushed angrily. "You never give up, do you? I didn't kill Cleo. You said Derek Hale was either playing detective or practicing blackmail.

Maybe it's simpler than that. Maybe he killed my sister. Did you ever stop to think about that?"

Only about once every minute since Derek's death, Frank thought. He wasn't about to let Miramba know that. Or to let her off the hook. "First, a catatonic, now a dead boy. Who will you point the finger at next, Miramba?"

Without warning, she reached for a vase at her elbow and threw it. It barely missed his head.

The Doberman inched forward. Frank eyed him warily. He stood. "You missed."

Her recovery was quick. Her tone became seductive again. "You know what your problem is? You want me, but you're not man enough to admit it."

He threw up his hands. "Please, spare me the melodramatics."

"Melodramatics! You think I'm acting?"

"I think you're always acting."

She placed her feet on the ground exposing tawny flesh. She came so close he could feel her breath on his cheeks. "Humor me, Damien. Admit it. There were moments when you wanted me. Fess up."

Frank shook his head. "Not one," he lied.

"Bastard," she screamed. "There are men who would kill for what I just offered you. I'll get even. I'll have your badge."

He smiled at her. "No, you won't. You won't do anything."

She reached for a silver and gold cigarette case, extracted a cigarette and lit it with a matching lighter. "Maybe. Maybe not. Why don't I let you worry about it for a while?" She blew smoke in his face. I'll have the maid show you out."

"Don't bother. I know my way out."

She smiled. "I bet you do. This surely isn't the first place you've been thrown out of." She turned her back on him.

In spite of everything, Frank admired her spirit. She was fire and she was ice. She was bitch and she was seductress. And she was unique.

Was she guilty of murder?

And if she was, could he ever hope to prove it?

CHAPTER 15

Frank drove by the house on Chapparral. Instinct told him that Marian was inside, grieving, with no one to comfort her. He felt an onus of guilt that was almost unbearable. He almost stopped, but forced himself to keep on driving, looking in his rear view mirror until the house disappeared from sight.

There had been other names on Derek's list. Beck was dead. Sheila might as well be. That left Jed Hale.

The apartment building had been given a sloppy new coat of paint, but weeds grew up between the cracks in the sidewalk, and the place still reeked of poverty. It was hard to adjust to a place like this one in a town where as many millionaires lived as lived in Beverly Hills. Frank once again longed to be back in New York where the dividing lines between rich and poor were more distinct, and in his mind more honest.

Hale answered the door. A wave of unclean air slapped Frank in the face. Hale's breath reeked of cheap whisky. He was quite drunk.

His words were slurred. "Well, come on in, Detective. Come join the wake. Of course you know about Derek?"

Frank nodded. "I could say I was sorry, and I'd mean it, but I don't think you'd care."

Hale snorted. "You'd be right. You bastards killed him. I loved that boy. I was more father to him than my brother ever thought about being." He paused, frowning at the half empty whisky bottle in his hand. "At least I was before my life went down the toilet and the bottle became my best friend."

"That's why I'm here. Derek had a list of names and addresses on him when he was killed. Your name was on that list. When did you see him last?"

Hale hiccupped. "The day before he took off."

"No good, Hale. He's been in the area recently. He was at the beach house, and I think he came to see you."

"Prove it."

"Why're you so defensive? The kid is dead. I think he was at the beach house the night of the murders. He may have seen something. He may have seen you there."

Hale laughed. "Come on, give me a break. I told you, I was glad someone killed Everett. Grateful to the son of a bitch, but I didn't kill Everett myself.

"I know that. Doug Beck killed him. He confessed before he died."

"Then what the fuck…"

"Someone else killed Cleo."

Hale staggered to the tiny kitchen. He turned on the faucet and splashed water on his face. "I'm under the weather. Drunk, you know. I could have sworn you said that someone else killed Cleo."

"I did. There were two murderers at the beach house that night."

"Two? You mean me and Beck? I never knew him, and why in the hell would I kill Cleo? I didn't have anything against her. Not really."

That was a definite problem with fingering Hale as Cleo's killer, Frank admitted. Hale had no real motive for killing her, unless…

"Would you say you would have done anything to protect your nephew?"

A guarded look passed over his drunken-bloated face. "I may be drunk, Damien, but I'm not stupid. I know what you're getting at. I didn't kill Cleo to protect Derek. I had no reason to, because Derek didn't kill my brother, and I never thought he did. I wasn't within miles of the place that night."

" Let's say I buy that. What I don't buy however is that you haven't seen Derek recently. What did he come here to tell you?"

The guarded look intensified. "Nothing, because Derek wasn't here."

Frank sensed that Hale was lying. Just as he knew that whatever Jed Hale was hiding, important or not, was a secret that Hale would never reveal.

Not to him, anyway.

***

Tom found Frank deep in thought, the inner office phone at his elbow ringing furiously. He picked up the receiver and handed it to Frank. "It's for you. Captain Markham."

Frank glanced up. "Sorry, I didn't hear it ringing. He took the instrument from Tom and said, "Sure. I'll be right there."

"He wants to see me in his office." He handed Tom a half-written report. "Be a pal and finish this for me, will you?"

A few minutes later he was in Markham's office.

"Sit down, Frank." Markham ordered.

Frank figured his being here had to do with the captain's visit to Marian. He was half right.

"Marian Hale took the death of her son rather well, Frank. Do you think she needs someone? Someone to stay with her, perhaps?"

"I can call her daughter. Marian doted on the boy. She's probably in shock. I guess I should go see her, but the last time I was there, it was anything but friendly. We argued about Derek."

"I see. Well, do whatever you think is right. What about the Hale case."

Frank gave him a surprised look. "The Hale case? I thought you'd written it off."

Markham sighed. "I had, but I was wrong. Every case deserves a just conclusion, and it deserves effort. You were the only one willing to give this case either. You're a good cop, Frank."

Frank suspected that somehow Markham knew he was planning to return to New York. Momentary anger was replaced by resignation. Whatever the reason for Markham's change of heart he was glad to know he wasn't alone anymore. He leaned forward eagerly. "I can't help but think that Derek's death, though an accident, was like finding a road map. All

I have to do is follow it. With Beck dead, and assuming he told the truth about not killing Cleo, we only have a handful of suspects. Derek himself, Miramba, Jed Hale, and Sheila Beck." He balled his fists. "I admit it's possible that Cleo's death was an accident? Unlike Everett Hale's death, I don't think killing her was planned or premeditated."

"What's your best guess, Frank?"

Frank sighed. "I don't have one yet. I want to go back to the beach house. I'd like to spend the night there. I think the house holds the key to everything. All I have to do is find which door it unlocks."

"Then go for it, Frank. You want Tom in on it?"

"No. I need to do this one alone."

"When will you leave for the beach house?"

"Right away. I've wasted too much time already."

***

It was almost dark. Frank sat in a chaise outside the beach house. He watched the final brilliant rays of a spectacular sunset. Hard to believe he thought, that just a few yards away two people had died so violently. He looked back at the house. He shuddered. If only it could tell what had happened within its walls that fateful night.

He sat outside long after darkness descended. Lights from distant offshore oil rigs dotted the darkened sea. A chill filled the air which went right to the bone, but not all of it was nature's work, Frank knew. Much of the chill he was experiencing came from within.

He stood and stared down at the rocks, their jagged edges outlined in the moonlight. It would take a sure-footed person to journey them at night. Beck had taken one hell of a chance when he'd chosen this way to leave here that night.

Frank made his way back to the house, opening the sliding glass doors that led to the living room. He delayed entering the master bedroom, taking a seat in the living room instead. He flipped on the knob of the giant television screen, then flipped it off. Get on with it, a voice inside him clamored to be heard. Do what you came here to do.

He retrieved his overnight bag from the entry hall and took it to the master bedroom and placed it on the bed. From here the view was just as commanding as it was from the living room, but the ocean vista no longer seemed serene, but menacing.

He wasn't tired but he decided to go to bed anyway. He took his toilet articles from the bag and carried them to the bathroom.

Cleo had died in here. What was she thinking about when she was attacked? Did the attack come as a surprise? Or, when she faced the intruder that night was she expecting violence?

He stroked his chin. There was enough stubble to warrant shaving, but what the hell, it could wait till morning. He brushed his teeth and cupped water in his hands and rinsed his face. He reached for a towel from one of the two neatly tiered rows of towels. A troubled expression crossed his face. A thought, barely formed and too vague was gone before the importance of it could take hold. He stared down at his hands. They were trembling. He grabbed the edge of the sink until his knuckles turned white.

Not now, he silently pleaded. Don't let me lose it now when I'm so close. With that swift thought came the realization that he was close to solving the Hale case. If only he could concentrate!

He pulled back the covers on the bed. He shivered. He'd been guilty just two days ago of thinking that whoever had slept here recently had a sense of the macabre. What was his being here making him?"

He crawled between the sheets and reached for the lamp beside the bed and turned off the light. It took a few seconds for him to adjust to the darkness. A chill ran down his spine. He wasn't alone in the room. The presence of others filled the darkness.

There was Everett Hale, a man he'd never met, but who he'd formed a pretty vivid mental picture of. He could feel the man's arrogance, and a touch of cruelty.

Cleo, a clone of her sister, Miramba. He sensed her need for adventure no matter what the personal risk.

And Michael Cordova.

Frank shot up in bed, sweat forming beads on his forehead. The others he could understand. Why Cordova?

Instead of fading, Cordova's presence not only filled the room, it overshadowed the presence of the two people who had reason to linger here, because they'd died here.

Frank turned on the light. He reached for a cigarette. Gradually, his heartbeat returned to normal. I should leave here, he thought, and knew that he couldn't

The answers he sought were here, or at least the roots of them.

He ground out his cigarette and turned out the light, willing the demons from within and those outside his influence to leave him.

He finally fell into a fitful sleep.

He awoke as dawn filtered its light into the bedroom. He dressed slowly, half afraid, half excited to face the day ahead. Pieces of the puzzle were haphazardly trying to fall into place giving him a fearsome headache.

His first stop was next door to one again talk to Sarah Meadows, because, as he'd jokingly remarked to Tom that first day, people like her often held the missing pieces and didn't know it.

All you had to do was ask the right questions.

***

Frank spent almost an hour with Sarah Meadows. She insisted on feeding him sweet rolls, orange juice and coffee. The unexpected treat of company for breakfast was too good for her to pass up. He impatiently listened to her idle chatter before getting down to business. He asked her if she'd seen anyone familiar at or near the beach house a few days before the Hales were killed. When he was through talking to her, she had no idea that she had handed him Cleo Hale's killer.

He called the crime lab crew to verify facts he'd been told at the onset of this case, aware that Sarah Meadows was hanging on his every word.

He returned to the house next door to gather his thoughts and map out his plan of action. He was in no hurry to proceed. Cleo's murderer wasn't going anywhere. He spent the next two hours sitting on the rocks below the Hale beach house, and thirty minutes inside the house before he left to tell Captain Markham what he'd learned.

Markham was attentive but skeptical. "Your theory makes sense, Frank, but your tangible proof is negligible. Missing prints?" He shook his head. "It's pretty thin. The rest is circumstantial."

Frank nodded. "I know."

"I'm with you all the way, Frank. I'll back you no matter which way you play it."

Markham's response was too little, too late. More, now than ever, Frank knew he didn't belong here. "I'm going back to New York when this is over, Cliff."

"There's nothing I can say to change your mind?"

"No , but thanks for wanting to."

"Our loss, Frank. You want to keep riding this thing out alone, or do you want Tom with you this time?"

Frank shook his head. "I already made the mistake once of sending a boy to do a man's job. It's time for me to correct that mistake, and I have to do it alone. If I'd questioned Sarah Meadows myself in the first place I could have saved a lot of people a lot of grief."

Yourself included, Markham thought. Out loud, he said, "Let me know if you need anything."

***

Frank stood in front of the house on Chapparral. He sensed that Marian knew he was here before he rang the doorbell.

She answered immediately. Hostility clashed with her need to se him. Her need won out. "Come in, Frank. I was just calling the funeral home. It's the first time I've been able to tackle it. Joanna is on her way home. Her plane gets in early tomorrow morning. She'll be here for the funeral."

"I'm sorry about Derek."

She gave him a questioning look. "Are you? You never liked him, and you and your kind killed him."

Frank sighed. His kind! He shouldn't be this surprised at her hostility, but it was going to get worse before it got better.

"You want something, Frank? A beer or a drink?"

He licked his lips. He could sure use one. He shook his head. "Not now."

"I think I'll have a drink. Funny, I've always been just a social drinker, but since I heard about Derek it's all I seem to want to do. Are funerals considered social occasions, do you think?"

She was close to the edge, and he was about to take her closer.

"I don't know." He waited for her to pour herself a drink. "Why didn't you tell me that the man who wouldn't and couldn't marry you was Doug Beck?"

Her drink spilled onto the freshly vacuumed carpet. "What did you say?"

"You and Doug Beck. You said you were discreet, but you were better than that, you kept your affair with him a secret from everybody. Well, almost everybody."

Her face turned a sick shade of gray. "I don't know what you're talking about."

"Sure you do. You were very careful not to be seen with him, and you were only discovered once. At the beach house."

"I still don't know what you're talking about."

" I'll spell it out for you. I made the mistake of having Tom talk to Sarah Meadows at the beginning of this case when I should have been doing it myself. I knew what the value of someone like her is to a case. All you have to do is keep them on track. I should have talked to her then," he reiterated. "The murders were fresher then, and so was I. Later, when I finally talked to her, I, too, almost missed a very vital statement she made. She repeated, as she had to Tom, that she'd seen Beck at the beach house with Mrs. Hale. It was reasonable to assume that she meant Cleo. Then I remembered her saying that Mrs. Hale had given her a key. Cleo wouldn't have done that. I checked with the realtor. You gave Sarah Meadows a key."

"My God, Frank! Of course I gave the woman a key. Someone needed to keep an eye on the house. There were two Mrs. Hales. Myself and Cleo. So, I don't see your point."

"Stay with me, and you will. I stayed at the beach house last night trying to get in touch with who was there, and what had happened there. It came to me that a woman like Sarah Meadows would have nothing but scorn for someone like Cleo. I was right. For her, you were Mrs. Hale. Cleo was "that woman." She confirmed it this morning. It was you she saw with Beck, not Cleo."

"Cleo was the one who was having an affair with Doug! You know that's true!"

Frank smiled. "She wasn't the only one, and that's the second time you've slipped and called him Doug. I missed that, too, the first time around. Cleo was having an affair with him, but that was before and after you. I think he dropped you for her. I think that's why you handed him to me that first day. You wanted to hurt him as much as he'd hurt you. You took one hell of a chance. What if Beck turned the tables and started talking about his affair with you? After that first lie to me about not knowing him, there was no way back for you, was there? That was foolish, Marian. The truth is always easier." He shrugged. "Not for you, I guess. Worrying about his giving you away must have kept you awake at night."

She swallowed the last of her drink. "This is silly. You wanted names. I gave you his. It was reasonable to assume he would want to harm Ev, and he did."

"Yes, he did, but you didn't believe that the first day I came to see you. I saw the look on your face when I told you he'd confessed to killing your ex-husband. You thought Derek killed his father. You thought that right up until the night I told you about Beck's confession."

She sank into a chair. She covered her face with her hands. "My affair with Doug wasn't relevant to the case, and yet it haunted me. You're right about that. Every day he could expose me as a liar. I still wonder why he didn't."

"He might have," Frank interrupted. "The night he died I think he was going to spill everything. He died before he could. You were afraid of that, weren't you? That's why when I told you he'd confessed to killing Everett Hale, you wanted to know what else he'd told me."

She seemed not to have heard him. "If you'd questioned my honesty, you'd have started to question everything else about me. I was so ashamed of my affair with him. It was short-lived and it was meaningless and ugly. He used me to get at Cleo. I felt unclean when it was over. You're right about Derek, too. I did think he killed his father, but I didn't suspect him of killing Cleo."

Frank took a deep breath. "Of course you didn't, because you knew better. You killed Cleo, Marian."

"Me! My God Frank, think about what you're saying!"

"You think I haven't. You're the only one left that make sense."

Her tone was guarded. "Then you have no proof."

"None that I can take to the D.A. that he will use. You did it, didn't you?" Agony filled his voice. "Why, Marian? Why did you kill her?"

Indecision lined her face making her look ten years older. "Oh, Frank, why couldn't I have met you sooner? Where were you when Ev turned his back on me? Where were you when Doug threw me away like yesterday's garbage? Where were you?" Tears welled up in her eyes, then ran unchecked down her cheeks.

"Don't do this, Marian. Don't make me feel guilty. I'm not responsible for your past or your mistakes." He grasped her by the shoulder, forcing her to look at him. "I want to know why you killed Cleo."

She wiped her eyes with the sleeve of her blouse, an uncharacteristically sloppy gesture for her, a further sign of how out of control she really was.

"How did you know it was me?" she whispered.

Until this moment he hadn't been one hundred percent sure. It could have been Derek. Frank's heart dropped all the way to his stomach. He'd never wanted to be wrong more than now, at this moment. He'd wanted her to deny everything, and if she had, a part of him knew he would have wanted to let it go.

His voice when he spoke was husky with emotion. "It was a lot of things. The neatness of the bedroom and the bathroom. Especially, the bathroom. The towels were stacked hotel style. You worked in one as a young girl. I bet if I checked in your linen closet the towels are neatly stacked in sets of bath towel, hand towel and washcloth."

The look on her face told him he was right.

"Such a simple thing. Bathroom towels. So simple it got by me. Keeping your affair with Beck wasn't the only information you kept from me. You were at the beach house a few days before the murders. Sarah Meadows saw you walking on the beach, and later driving away from the house. It always bothered me why there were no prints in the house. Why wipe the whole house clean? Logic dictated that whoever killed Everett and Cleo Hale was only in the bedroom and the bathroom and probably wore gloves. Yet the whole house was clean of prints, and the cleaning people hadn't been there in almost a week. I think you were in a state of panic that night and wanted to wipe all traces of your presence there, so you took no chances that prints from days before might incriminate you in any way, or Derek either for that matter. I'm sure that later you must have realized the folly of that move. It would have been easier for you to admit you were there a few days earlier, then your prints wouldn't have meant a thing. Their not being there turned out to be more incriminating in the end."

Frank paused. He wasn't happy to have solved the mystery of Cleo's murder. "Whoever wiped the place clean would have worried about their prints being identified. The field of suspects narrowed when Doug Beck died with a confession on his lips, and none of the other suspects were at or near the beach house for weeks before the murders took place. Finally, when I stayed at the beach house last night one thing kept climbing to the top. The house was neat and orderly. Like you. Like the murder scene. Your affair with Beck gave you the motive I've been hunting for."

"You think I killed her because of Doug!"

"Not entirely. Why did Derek run away, Marian? Did he know you'd committed murder?"

"No! I mean I'm not sure. I think he was there earlier than he claimed to have been. He may have seen me leaving. That isn't why he left home. He left because when I found Cleo's ring in his room, I accused him of killing Ev. He vehemently denied it, but I refused to believe him. I demanded he give me the ring. He wouldn't do it. I decided to let him sleep on it. The next day he was gone."

"Why did you think Derek killed his father?"

"Because Ev had given him reason to. The night Ev was killed Derek didn't come home. I waited for him. I waited until almost one-thirty in the morning before I began to panic." She laughed, the sound hollow. "I was afraid of what I might do. Not to Cleo, but to Ev."

"Why Everett?"

Anger sparked her tear-filled eyes. "I painted a pretty bright picture of life after Ev. It was a façade. All of us, myself, Joanna, and especially Derek, suffered from Ev's rejection of us. We could have handled another affair. We were used to them. Then along came Cleo. Young , beautiful, and black, and he married her. Until then I'd never considered myself to be a bigot. Maybe most of us aren't until we're tested. His marriage cut us off, made us feel like castoffs. We all pretended to adjust, me with my clandestine affair with Cleo's ex-lover, which seemed like poetic justice at the time, Derek with an indifference he didn't feel. Only Joanna took it all in stride."

She sighed. "Poor Derek. Under all the concealed anger was a son's admiration for a father and a need for acceptance. The two emotions were in such conflict, it was a hard thing for an adolescent to deal with. Two days before Ev and Cleo...before they died, Ev called here. Derek was planning on spending the weekend with him at the beach house. Ev told me he thought it would be better if Derek stayed away. My son, his son, made Cleo nervous. My son made the bitch nervous! I couldn't believe Ev's insensitivity. I pleaded with him to reconsider. He wouldn't listen to me. He went even further. He and Cleo had decided that Derek shouldn't visit him at all any more, he said. I was to explain to Derek that Ev would come here to see the children when he could get away." She sneered in disgust. "He didn't even have the courage to tell Derek himself."

She couldn't have known, Frank thought, that all Cleo wanted was to make sure that she and Everett Hale were alone at the beach house that weekend. Otherwise, her plan with Beck wouldn't work. A part of Frank, the part of him that had loved Marian, wanted to reach out to her. To take her in his arms. He forced himself to stay detached. "You told Derek about the call?"

"I had no choice. It would have been harder for him to have been thrown out of his father's house. Ev left no doubt in my mind that Cleo would stoop to that if she had to."

Marian moved away from him. "When I told him, Derek was angrier than I'd ever seen him before. He made threats. I didn't take him seriously. Who ever does? When I came home that night and found Derek's bed empty, I was filled with apprehension. At one thirty, I took the car and drove to the beach community. The security guard was in a drunken stupor as usual. I parked my car outside the gate and walked in, using my code to open the gate."

She glanced back at Frank. Her eyes were dry now. "Should I have a lawyer present, do you think?" She avoided his uncompromising expression. "No , of course not. You're willing to play judge and jury, aren't you?" She said harshly. "I used my key to open the front door," she went on, her voice shaky. She wrung her hands together. "I crept into the bedroom. I looked over at the bed. Ev was so still. When I moved closer I saw he was dead."

She gasped, the pain of that night returning. "I went there in hopes of warding off trouble. I was devastated because I was too late."

Frank frowned. "Didn't it occur to you that someone other than Derek had killed your ex-husband?"

She flushed. "No. I wish it had. I looked desperately around the room for Cleo. She wasn't in the bedroom. I moved to the window and stared out into the night. I saw a figure on the rocks. I was sure it was Derek."

Marian had been the figure at the window Beck had mistake for Cleo, Frank thought, and coincidentally, he'd been as wrong as Marian in identifying a shadowy outline. "It was Beck you saw," Frank responded. "Where was Derek while all this was taking place?"

She gave him a disoriented look. "Derek? I don't know where he was. He told me later that he had spent the night walking the beach and ended up at the beach house at dawn, but I think he was lying. I think he was there earlier and waited until dawn to call the police. He was probably frightened."

Derek thought back to the day he'd first met Derek. He hadn't seemed frightened. Just the opposite. He'd seemed almost exhilarated.

As if anxious to tell it all, she went on, "I heard a moan. It came from the bathroom."

Frank swallowed air. His lungs seemed incapable of taking breath. In spite of everything that had been said so far he hadn't been able to stop hoping that at the last minute she'd some up with an explanation of Cleo's death that he could live with. Hope of that now left him.

Marian, now that she had begun to talk about the events of the night at the beach house, couldn't seem to stop. "Cleo sat on the floor of the bathroom, her hand against her head." Her words were slurred. "All I could think of was that she could send my son to prison. There was a statue in the bathroom. Cleo used it as a soap dish. Unconsciously, I picked it up. I think I might not have used it, or killed her if she hadn't started to taunt me. "It's the slime-bag's mother," she said. "My God, what did Everett ever see in you, or Doug? Especially, Doug. He made love to you to make me jealous. He never cared about you. Never." At that moment, I wasn't sure who I hated more, Cleo or Doug. Reason left me, and blind rage took over. Madness, really. I hit her with the soap dish. She gave me a look of disbelief and staggered over to the shower. She put out her hands for support. She fell inside. I was desperate. Now, she could not only hurt Derek, but she could incriminate me, too. I took the statue and I hit her again and again until all I could see was her blood."

Frank felt sick. He knew now that his attraction to her from the onset was not her resemblance to Claire but the danger she represented. Like Cordova, he'd been attracted to her like a moth to a flame. Who are the really sick ones? He wondered. Them or me?

Tears ran freely down Marian's cheek. "There was so much blood. I wrapped her in the shower curtain and dragged her into the bedroom. I had to stop several times to catch my breath. I hadn't come there to kill anyone, so I had to improvise. It seemed like a good idea to confuse the issue, to make the crime scene so complicated it would seem beyond a teenage imagination so that Derek wouldn't look like a serious suspect.

"Cleo was tiny. She only weighed ninety pounds. Dragging her to the bed, she felt more like nine hundred. I placed her in the bed beside Ev so as to look like they were killed together. There was something wrong with the picture." She grimaced. "Cleo's face was a mess. She wasn't human anymore. She was…she was a thing, like a broken doll. Ev looked almost peaceful. I had to match his injuries with those I'd dealt to Cleo. There was a hammer by the bed. It had bloodstains on it. I was angry with Derek. Leaving it behind was careless. I turned away from Ev and I smashed his skull over and over again."

"I tried to tell myself that this was a nightmare that I'd wake up from any minute," Marian sobbed. "When that didn't happen, I began to systematically clean up the beach house. I scrubbed the bedroom floor, the tiles in the bathroom, and the shower walls. I wiped every surface in the house twice to be sure, even the front gate. I worked in a frenzy, worried that if I didn't get away from there soon, I would be discovered. I put out fresh towels at the last minute. It was a silly thing to do, but it was a reflex action. I kept wondering if Derek's state of mind matched my own. I left, after once again wiping any surface that I'd remembered touching. I took the shower curtain, the hammer and the statue with me. I took the old beach road and stopped and threw them in the ocean. I trembled all the way home. When I got there, Joanna was still a sleep, but Derek still hadn't returned."

Marian rubbed her arms. She was rambling, at times her voice so low Frank had to strain to hear her. "I tried to wash Cleo's blood from me. I used the downstairs shower so as not to awaken Joanna, even though she's a sound sleeper. It used to annoy me when she was a child and she had a hard time waking up and getting ready for school. All through high school she battled tardiness. I found myself grateful for that trait." Marian increased the tension on her arms. "I scrubbed my skin until it hurt, but no matter how hard I tried, I couldn't wash away the events of the night. I sat up in a chair waiting for Derek to return. The hours passed. Dawn turned into morning. The first I knew of Derek's whereabouts was when your partner called to tell me that he'd discovered the bodies, and that you wished to talk to all of us."

Frank remained silent...and miserable.

Marian whirled around. "For God's sake, Frank, say something."

Weariness filled Frank's voice. "I can't think of a thing to say to you, except I thought I loved you."

"Thought! You did love me, Frank. You do love me."

He felt sorry for her. Angry with himself. "It wasn't love, Marian. It was something unhealthy and unbalanced. As unhealthy and unbalanced as my near friendship with Cordova. I fooled myself into thinking you reminded me of Claire, when all the time it was him."

She frowned. "I don't understand."

"I know, but I do. That's the problem."

Her eyes took on a wild look. "You're going to leave me! You're just like all the others, my mother, Ev, Doug. Even Derek left me." Abruptly, she was unnaturally calm. "Will you turn me in?"

Frank hadn't thought past this moment.

"I'm burying my son tomorrow," she said. "At least give me that much time."

He nodded. "I'll give you that."

"Let me help you understand how it was," she pleaded.

"Understand what?" he shouted. "You damn near destroyed me. That scene you set at the beach house placed me in another time zone. You brought Cordova back into my life. Not only with your theatrics, but the aura you, yourself exuded. I lost my cutting edge. My instincts were clouded. From the first day I met you, I was on a roller coaster ride I couldn't get off, and didn't know why. Claire tried to warn me. She, unlike me, sensed the danger you represented. Damn, I was stupid. That's why marriage was so important to you, wasn't it? You needed my protection in case I discovered the truth about you."

"No! Maybe it was that way in the beginning, but as time went on, loving you became a way of life. It took precedence over everything. Derek, my own survival, everything."

For a moment he believed her, but how and what she felt for him now was no longer important.

***

The pier was only sparsely occupied. There was a chill in the air, but Frank didn't feel it. On his way here he'd mailed an account of his conversation with Marian to Cliff Markham. Marian was Markham's problem now. Frank stared down at the water below. It seemed to beckon him. For a few precarious seconds he pondered how blissfully simple it would be to let the sea take him as its own.

He shook his head to clear it, oblivious of the curious glances of two old men fishing off the end of the pier. His last conversation with Marian came rushing back to him. Like Cordova, she'd subconsciously wanted to be found out. Most basically decent murderers did.

Frank extracted his badge from inside his jacket. He stared at his reflection in the brass surface. The badge represented a way of life, one he felt removed from. It seemed tarnished, like his life. He placed it on the wooden railing. He buried his head in his hands; then he lifted his head and deliberately and determinedly threw the symbol of his career into the ocean below.

Frank walked over to his car parked a few yards away. He started the engine. He checked the gas gauge. He had a full tank. Enough gas to take him far, far away from here.

He drove off the pier and headed south on the freeway. It didn't seem important to decide on a destination.

There would be time for that later. For now, it only seemed important to put distance between himself and Marian Hale.

***

For the first two weeks Frank just kept driving in an eastward direction. He ended up in Atlantic City, cashed in on the line of credit on his master charge and visa cards, and engaged himself in mindless gambling. For a while, maybe because he didn't care, he found himself on a winning streak. When the streak turned on him, and he was down to his last few dollars, he took a job in security at one of the casinos.

The cop in him refused to curl up and die. Three months after he'd left Santa Barbara, Frank returned to New York. He had a long talk with Captain Jenkins, his old superior. He told him everything. The way he'd felt after Claire was brutalized, his fear that someone would discover he near mental collapse, the Hale case, and the similarities to the Cordova killings that he'd only imagined, the undercurrent that had dominated him, and finally, he told Jenkins about Marian.

"You're a good and decent cop, Frank," Jenkins said. "Like a lot of good cops, you lost your way. What happened to Marian Hale by the way?"

"She's dead. I called Cliff Markham about two weeks after I left Santa Barbara," Frank went on. "I was finally allowing myself to think about Marian again. Pain filled his eyes. "I could think about her without hating her for what she almost did to me, but I was still angry. As much with myself as with her. I wondered what kind of person I was. I liked Cordova before I found out what he was and what he'd done, and I loved Marian. Great, huh? A serial killer and a woman who had it in her to beat two people to a pulp! Anyway, her death was an accident." Frank shrugged. "At least that's the official cause of death. Two days after she buried Derek, her car went over a cliff on Highway 1. There were no other cars involved."

"Suicide?"

Frank shook his head. "I'll never know. Could be she saw it as the only way out. I've thought a lot about what happened. I think she went to the beach house that night looking for an excuse to harm Cleo. She was sick and hurt inside. All her life people had left her behind, and finally, something snapped." He sighed. "Even I left her."

"You have nothing to blame yourself for, Frank." Jenkins said.

"Hell, I quit blaming myself a while back. No future in it. Anyway, she was lost long before I met her. She said she wished she'd met me sooner. It's the one thing she said I can never forget. I can't help thinking about how different our lives might have been for both of us if…" He shrugged. "That's another time, another life. I'm ready to come back to work now, Captain."

Jenkins gave him a speculative look. "After all you've told me, I can't let you back on the streets right away, Frank. You're going to have to prove yourself all over again."

Frank nodded dismally. "I know that."

Jenkins sighed. "You know more about the streets than most of us have forgotten. You were raised on them. You're in a position to do us a real service. You can teach green cops, some of them on the streets for the first time, how to survive out there. You could save their lives."

"Are you offering me a desk job, Captain?"

Jenkins nodded. "For the time being. If you're only half the man I think you are, it won't be for ever."

Frank wanted to argue that he was ready to go back on the streets now, but a voice of reason from inside of him told him that Jenkins was right to put him behind a desk for a while. He needed time to let the wounds heal. All the wounds.

Surprisingly, the job of teacher, mentor, and guardian angel wasn't as hard to take as Frank had expected, but he still hungered for the sound and smells of the streets.

He'd make it back out there, he vowed. After he'd earned the right, paid his dues again, and proven he was as sound as any man in the department. It would take time. That, Frank acknowledge, was something of which he had plenty.

END

CPSIA information can be obtained
at www.ICGtesting.com
Printed in the USA
FSHW010642031218
54199FS